BRAND: BROTHERHOOD OF EVIL

Infiltrating an organisation dedicated to the resurrection of the Confederacy, and putting a stop to their planned uprising, places Jason Brand in the firing line on his new assignment. As Brand becomes involved with the fanatical St. Clair family, violence erupts and he has a fight for survival on his hands. Brand makes his stand against the rebels, uncovers an assassination plot — and suffers a very personal tragedy of his own . . .

Books by Neil Hunter
in the Linford Western Library:

BODIE:
TRACKDOWN
BLOODY BOUNTY
HIGH HELL
THE KILLING TRAIL
HANGTOWN
THE DAY OF THE SAVAGE

BRAND:
GUN FOR HIRE
HARDCASE
LOBO
HIGH COUNTRY KILL
DAY OF THE GUN

NEIL HUNTER

BRAND: BROTHERHOOD OF EVIL

Complete and Unabridged

LINFORD
Leicester

First Linford Edition
published 2000

British Library CIP Data

Hunter, Neil
    Brand 6.—Brotherhood of evil—
Large print ed.
Linford western library
1. Western stories
2. Large type books
I. Title
823.9'14 [F]

ISBN 0–7089–5755–2

Published by
F. A. Thorpe (Publishing)
Anstey, Leicestershire

Set by Words & Graphics Ltd.
Anstey, Leicestershire
Printed and bound in Great Britain by
T. J. International Ltd., Padstow, Cornwall

This book is printed on acid-free paper

1

Deputy United States Marshal Jack Doyle cursed silently, but with genuine feeling. He was cold, wet and damned uncomfortable. He wished he was back in Dallas instead of being stuck in Galveston. In Dallas there was that redheaded half-Irish girl called Kelly. The one with the body of an angel and breasts like ripe melons. Doyle groaned at the memory, and tried to push the image of the girl out of his mind. It took some doing and by the time he'd rid himself of her tantalising picture he felt distinctly worse off. The rain felt even wetter and colder. The wind cut through his sodden clothing with sadistic force. He hunched further into the corner, blinking rain from his eyes and stared across the glistening street at the US Government warehouse. Beyond the dark bulk of the building the oily waters of Galveston Bay broke heavily against the sodden pilings of the wharf.

Fishing his watch from his pocket Doyle strained his eyes to peer at the face. It had gone midnight and he was beginning to wonder whether his information had been false. There was only one way to find out. That entailed staying exactly where he was and waiting some more. These days it seemed he spent a great deal of his time sitting around waiting for things to happen. He dragged a thin cigar from his pocket and stuck it between his lips. It was only as he searched for a match that he realised what he was doing. Doyle snatched the cigar from his mouth and tossed it aside. He jerked the dripping brim of his hat lower over his face and pulled his coat closer around his neck. It failed to stop cold fingers of rain sneaking down his back.

He saw the wagon before he heard the muted sound of its approach. Pulled by a pair of rain-slick horses it rolled slowly along the wharf. A dark canvas sheet covered the rear of the wagon. Doyle counted two men on the seat up front, with three more sitting near the rear.

The wagon rolled right up to the warehouse and drew to a creaking halt. One of the men up front climbed down and walked straight to the doors of the warehouse. There was no hesitation or fumbling. The man produced a key and opened the heavy padlock securing the doors. He dragged the doors open and waved the driver of the wagon to move forward. The wagon rolled inside the warehouse and the doors were swiftly drawn to behind it.

A bead of sweat rolled down Doyle's face. His informant had been right. What he had forgotten to mention was that these people were professionals. Too professional. The way they had entered the warehouse spoke of men with a single purpose. The kind who wouldn't allow anyone to get in their way. If a problem arose they would deal with it as easily as they had got into the warehouse.

Jack Doyle felt his lips go dry. He was no coward. Neither was he reckless. He knew and accepted the dangers of his profession. That didn't mean he had to like them. But he knew he had to overcome his feelings and get closer to these people. He had to find out what they were after.

He pushed his coat back and reached for the heavy Colt holstered on his right hip. His fingers touched the cold butt in the same instant something hard was jammed into his back.

'Leave it, bucko, or I'll put a hole through you here and now!'

The voice alone got the message across. Doyle took his hand away from his gun and felt someone lift it from the holster.

'Seeing as you're so interested we'll go over and join my friends,' the unseen man said. 'Walk ahead of me and do it steady so's I don't get nervous on this trigger.'

4

The walk to the warehouse seemed endless. Doyle found he was wishing it would never end. There was a growing feeling inside him that warned he would find nothing pleasant inside the place. He didn't rule out the possibility of dying. These men wouldn't want the knowledge of what they were doing being spread around. Once they realised that Doyle was a Marshal they would certainly want him kept quiet. The most permanent way of ensuring that would be to kill him.

Doyle knew the risks of his business. He'd known from the day he pinned on the badge. His instructors had laid it on the line right from day one.

'Don't expect that badge to bring you anything but trouble! You want gratitude go join a Sunday School! You want fame join a circus! All this job will bring you is a boot in the crutch and a bullet in the back of your head up some dark alley!'

That was what they had told him. And a great deal more. Like every other operative who joined the department Jack Doyle hadn't been looking for gratitude or fame. Just the chance to do a damn good job for his own satisfaction.

The problem was that right now that bullet in the back of the head was starting to look entirely possible.

As Doyle paused outside the warehouse his captor rapped on the door. After a few seconds the door eased open and a man's face gleamed briefly in subdued lamplight.

'Inside, bucko.'

Doyle stepped inside. The area close to the door was dark. A block of angular shadows. Beyond was a pool of light. Shapes moving around the parked wagon.

Behind Doyle someone spoke urgently, the voice too low for him to pick out the words.

'Go on,' Doyle's captor snapped, thrusting the gun against Doyle's spine.

Reaching the wagon Doyle saw one of the dark figures step forward. He got an impression of a tall, broad man, his shape muffled by a heavy topcoat. The face was obscured by the upturned collar. Only the eyes showed clearly. Cold and bright, they shone with a brittle hardness that was without feeling. Doyle sensed evil in those eyes and he knew there was nothing good in this situation for him.

'Who is he?' The eyes never wavered from Doyle's face.

'Let's find out!'

Another man pushed forward. He was tall and lean, with pale blond hair and a soft look to his finely chiselled features. He walked with a limp, favouring his stiff left leg. He glared at Doyle with ill-concealed hostility as his slender, woman's hands searched through the Deputy's pockets.

Jack Doyle tensed. Nerves strung tight. Waiting for the moment when they discovered his identity.

'Damn!' The blond man stepped back. He held up Doyle's badge. 'Now what do we do?' His voice was edged with the beginnings of panic.

The man in the topcoat leaned forward.

'Was he alone, Royce?'

'He was, Colonel.' This came from the man who had brought Doyle inside. He spoke with assurance.

'How do we know he didn't tell others where he was going?' the blond said, his control slipping even more.

'That might be true, Colonel,' the one named Royce agreed.

The Colonel was silent for a moment. He gaze moved to a spot beyond Doyle's left shoulder. 'It appears this is something you should handle, Royce.'

'Yes, sir,' Royce said.

Hell no!

Jack Doyle's silent protest was followed by instant action. He knew exactly what the Colonel meant, and realised that he had nothing to lose and everything to gain.

He dropped to a crouch, taking him below the level of the gun at his back, twisting his body round. As he faced about he lunged forward, slamming shoulder-first into Royce. He heard the man curse, then felt the whack of Royce's gun barrel as it slammed across the side of his head. Doyle stumbled, regained his footing, and pushed forward again, hammering his fists at Royce's body. Royce spun away from him, crashing into a stack of crates and toppling sideways. Doyle heard the scrape of a boot close by and turned towards it. It was the blond, the gleam of steel in his hand. Doyle didn't hesitate, and instead of pulling back he advanced. His swinging fist drove into the pale face. The blond man uttered a shrill yell as the blow landed. Stepping away from the moaning figure Doyle pushed past the muffled shape of the Colonel and made for the shadows beyond the spill of light.

Doyle ran. There was nothing else for him to do. He could hear the others behind him, yelling to each other as they followed. He regretted not knowing the layout of the warehouse as he crashed into objects. Stumbling, falling, picking himself up again he felt blood streaming down his face and a sudden stab of pain from bruised ribs. But he still kept running. He had to if he wanted to stay alive.

The voices behind him faded, then rose. Men swore in frustration. Doyle realised they were as confused as he was. The warehouse was unknown to them as well. It gave him an edge — albeit a slight one. Doyle stopped running and made an attempt at getting his bearings. He just wished he had his gun. At least then he would have had something to fight back with. Without his weapon he felt helpless. He edged his way along a stack of wooden crates, peering ahead of him.

Where was the door?

If he could get outside then maybe he could . . .

Ahead of him he made out a faint lessening in the darkness. A pale outline. Was it the door? He moved towards it, relieved when he saw he was passing the wagon. No one seemed to be near it. Perhaps they were all still behind him. In the depths of the warehouse

He reached the door. For a moment he was sure it was locked. But it swung open at his touch. Cold rain drifted in, chill against his face.

Doyle stepped outside. The moment he was on the street he began to run, ignoring the driving rain. He had to get away from the warehouse. Away from the men who wanted to kill him.

He didn't hear the shot. Just felt something strike his lower back. A heavy, numbing blow. The force of it knocked him to his knees. He landed hard, a pained cry bursting from his lips. It was then he knew he'd been shot. Pain flowered inside his body. He struggled to stand upright, fighting the onset of weakness that threatened to cripple him. On his feet again he staggered drunkenly, slumping against a wall. He clawed at the rough brick to stop from falling again. Then he heard a sound and turned.

It was the man called Royce. He stood in the middle of the street, a tight smile on his angular face. His flesh gleamed with rain and his black hair was plastered tightly to his skull. The big revolver in his hand rose slowly.

'Nowhere to run, boy!'

In that final moment Jack Doyle realised something that had been in his thoughts from the moment he had entered the warehouse. The man called Royce. The blond man. And the Colonel. They all spoke with the same accent.

Unmistakable.

A Southern drawl.

A pointless revelation now because Doyle wasn't going to be able to pass the information along. Nor would it save his life.

With a defiant yell Doyle shoved himself away from the wall, reaching out for Royce.

The muzzle of the revolver blossomed with flame and smoke. The sound of the shot this time was loud in Doyle's ears. It grew and grew, filling his skull, even drowning out the final scream that burst from his lips in protest against the pain in his chest. Doyle felt himself falling. Then he was down on the ground. The rain on his face felt odd, he couldn't move. Or make a sound. But he could still see.

The image that was imprinted on his mind just before everything went dark was of Royce looming over him. The big-boned face glistened wetly. The lips curved in a cold smile. But it was the odd, shining wildness in Royce's eyes that frightened Doyle even more than death in those final moments.

It was the burning stare of the fanatic!

2

Jason Brand crossed the tracks of the Galveston rail depot, making for the single, isolated Pullman coach standing in one of the sidings. The coach was painted in rich maroon and blue, every panel lined with thin gold-leaf gilding. It was a rich, impressive piece of exhibitionism. Brand wondered who it belonged to. Certainly not the man who was waiting inside for Brand.

Not Frank McCord.

True, he was using it to get to Brand, but the Chief of the Washington Law Department was not the kind of man to waste money on such a chunk of luxury.

McCord's telegram had come out of the blue, informing Brand that he would be arriving in Galveston the next day.

The man himself was standing on the

observation platform at the rear of the coach, watching Brand's approach.

'You're looking better than the last time I saw you,' McCord said.

'I feel a whole lot better,' Brand replied.

McCord led the way inside. They passed through to the Pullman's lounge. Part of it had been fitted out as an office, complete with oak desk and cabinets. Booklined shelves were fitted to the walls and a heavy safe stood in the far corner.

'Belongs to the owner of the railroad,' McCord explained. He eased into the leather chair behind the desk. 'He owed the Department a few favours.'

Brand tossed his hat down and stretched his lean frame into a comfortable armchair.

'Very impressive,' he murmered.

Frank McCord leaned forward. 'I don't use things to impress people, Brand. Just to serve a useful function.'

Brand glanced up from the cigar he

was lighting. 'That apply to people as well as furniture?' he asked.

McCord stared at him. Then a frosty smile edged his lips. 'That rest has certainly perked you up,' he said.

'Yeah,' Brand replied. He was thinking that the main reason for his full recovery had been Sarah Debenham. She had made all the difference. He glanced at McCord and knew instinctively that his vacation was over. McCord hadn't come all this way simply to pass the time of day with him.

'I have a copy of your latest medical,' McCord said. 'According to it you are fully recovered and fit for duty.'

'I could have told you that without the medical,' Brand said. As good as the relationship had been with Sarah, he needed the challenge a new assignment would offer.

'Good,' McCord said. He instantly became businesslike. A folder was produced and opened on the desk in front of McCord.

'What do you know about an organisation calling itself *The Brotherhood of the Confederacy?*'

'Nothing.'

McCord tapped the file. 'When you have read this you'll know as much as anyone outside the group.'

He passed the file across to Brand and watched him study the contents.

'Is this *the* St Clair?'

'Ex-Colonel. Now Senator Beauregard St Clair.' McCord leaned back in the leather chair. 'As far as we can tell he's the head of the Brotherhood. I don't have to remind you of his political leanings. St Clair is dyed-in-the-wool Southern. The war may be over but St Clair is still fighting the battle.'

'Twenty years on?'

McCord smiled. 'St Clair doesn't understand the concept of forgive and forget. He's as anti-Unionist now as he ever was. Maybe more so. He's had a lot of time to let his hate grow. Watching his part of the country being drawn into the Union way of things.

17

Seeing Yankee money and power taking over the Southland. Twenty years on and Beauregard St Clair still hates us. He's a fanatic of the worst kind. The most dangerous to have to deal with.'

'What does the Brotherhood have in mind?'

'I believe St Clair wants to establish a Confederate power group. Even a fighting force. With him as leader.'

'He might just do it,' Brand said. 'From what I know of the man he has a way with words. The kind that would appeal to sympathisers to his cause.'

'Read the reports. You'll understand what he's already doing.'

'Does St Clair know he's under suspicion?'

McCord shrugged. 'Maybe. Maybe not. St Clair is no fool. Most of our information comes courtesy of the US Secret Service. They've been watching St Clair for almost a year now. When they were certain of their facts they took them to the President. He called me in and we both decided it was enough to go on.'

Brand took another look at the reports contained in the file. Page after page of detailed information, telling of meetings, along with dates and times and places. And as much as possible about the people attending the meetings.

'One or two familiar names,' Brand observed.

'All fine Southern gentlemen,' McCord agreed. 'You will of course have noted that they are to a man both politically and commercially influential.'

'And not one of them short of a dollar.' Brand closed the file. 'Is there anything to add to what's in the file?'

'Three nights ago a Government warehouse here in Galveston, was broken into. I say broken. Actually the people who committed the crime had a key and simply let themselves in. When they left they took three brand new Gatling Guns, four cases of rifles and two of Colt revolvers. They also took ammunition for all three weapons.'

'Is there a connection to St Clair?'

'Yes. The same thing that connected the Brotherhood to a number of other robberies. St Clair was seen in Galveston two days before the robbery. He left the day after. I did some checking and the same applied to raids in EI Paso, Dallas and Austin.'

'Not too smart,' Brand said. 'Being around every time.'

'One of his failings. St Clair has to be in the thick of things. He has to be involved in all aspects of the Brotherhood.'

'Anything else about this raid I need to know?'

McCord's face hardened. 'A Deputy US Marshal named Jack Doyle had a tip something might be going to happen. He staked out the warehouse on his own. His body was found next morning. He'd been shot to death.'

'Not very brotherly,' Brand said.

'The general opinion is they're building up to something. I want you to find out what it is. Locate their headquarters. Put a stop to whatever they're up to. No quarter on this, Brand. Just end it.'

Brand said all right. This was exactly what he'd been waiting for.

'You want me to report in? Might not be possible if I get in too deep.'

McCord shook his head. 'I only want to hear from you to tell me it's all over. Try not to cause a national uprising. The idea is to stop a war — not start one. Just remember the President has put his name to this, so I do not want him being caused any embarrassment.'

'I'll do my best.' Brand stood up, smoothing the brim of his hat. 'I'll leave before you start to sing the anthem.'

'Give my regards to the young lady,' McCord said dryly, his final words hanging in the air as Brand walked out the door.

★ ★ ★

'Do you know Lucilla St Clair?'

'I have met her twice at social

21

functions. Why?'

Sarah Debenham glanced at Brand's reflection in the mirror of her dressing table.

'I'd like to meet her,' he said, and waited for her reaction.

'So do a lot of other men. Few ever make it.'

Sarah turned from the dressing table. studying him closely.

Brand returned her gaze with cool indifference.

'Answer me, Jason. Why do really want to meet her?'

Brand sighed. The trouble with intelligent women was that they were constantly exercising that intelligence. Tossing his hat on a chair he crossed the room to stare out of the window, looking down on the busy street. Raising his eyes he was able to see over the rooftops and catch a glimpse of the Bay, its water sparkling in the sunlight. Tall masts, festooned with ropes and canvas swayed with the roll of the ships at anchor.

'Is this to do with your work?' Sarah asked. Her tone was light but he could sense the subtle probing.

'Should it be?'

A smile touched her lovely lips. 'You receive a telegram out of the blue that sends you scurrying to a meeting with someone you won't name. Then you suddenly want to meet Lucilla St Clair, the daughter of a Senator known for his reputation as a fire eating rabble-rouser. All very mysterious.'

'No mystery,' Brand answered, but he knew she didn't believe him.

Sarah came to him. Slipped her arms around his neck.

'By the way, how is Mr McCord?'

This time Brand had to smile. She seemed able to read him without effort. Perhaps it was telling him they had been together too long. The fact that she seemed to know him so well left him with an uncomfortable feeling.

'Well?' she repeated.

'The same. McCord never changes.'

She studied him for a moment. Then

she said: 'I get the feeling you don't always approve of him.'

'What gave you that idea?' Brand was losing interest in McCord as a subject of conversation. Sarah's closeness. The sheer robe, her only covering, was arousing other, more basic thoughts in his mind.

'I am being serious,' she said. And then: 'Jason! Jason Brand, you stop that right now. Damn you, I'd feel a lot safer if I could see where your hands are . . . I mean . . . that is . . . oh my . . . *oh my*.'

Later she asked him the same question again. Lying beside her on the big bed he was totally relaxed now, his long, hard-muscled body warm against her own sleekly nude curves.

'I have to get close to someone,' he admitted. He was reluctant to involve her too deeply — but on the other hand she did have the connections to get him into the company of the St Clair family. 'Sarah, all I want you to do is get me an introduction to Lucilla St Clair. I'll take it from there.'

Sarah nudged him with a rounded hip. 'I'm sure you will.' She sat up, sweeping tousled hair away from her face. 'Maybe I need to know more if I'm going to help.'

Brand drew his appreciative gaze from her softly curved breasts. 'The less you know the less you can tell.'

'Gossip over the china teacups?' she said tartly.

'Sarah, the people I'm after are not a bunch of little old ladies. They've already murdered one man we know of. There could be others. I could do with your help, but I'll manage without if I have to.'

'Bully,' she scolded gently. 'You don't scare me, Jason Brand. Remember I knew you when you weren't so tough.'

She reached out to touch the puckered scar in his side. The place where Raven's bullet had gone in. She found her gaze drawn to the other scars marking his body, and for a moment she found herself wondering how it was possible for someone to carry so many reminders of past violence and still be alive. He existed in a world of brutal savagery, yet seemed to be able to live beneath the shadow and ignore the pain and suffering. Perhaps one day he would draw aside the curtain a little and let her look into his soul. Maybe then she would be able to understand what it was that drove him, pushing him into the pitiless glare of the spotlight, offering himself as a target for the hate and the eager guns of the savages. If that day ever did come it would be his decision — not hers.

She slipped off the bed and reached for her robe, drawing it across her shoulders. She was conscious of his gaze lingering openly on her nakedness. It didn't bother her. His uncomplicated appreciation of her loveliness flattered her, made her feel complete and at ease in his presence.

'I'll see what I can do about getting you that introduction to Lucilla.'

Brand sat up.

'I won't forget it.'

A slow smile edged her mouth. On an impulse she let the robe slip to the floor and eased back onto the bed.

'I know you won't,' she said. 'I'm not going to give you the opportunity to.'

She leaned over, her lips seeking his, the hard tips of her breasts brushing his chest as she reached for him.

3

Senator Beauregard St Clair clipped the end from a cigar rolled from fine Virginia leaf. He lit it slowly, deriving great satisfaction from the mellow, sweet aroma. He gazed across his huge oak desk at Parker Royce, seeing the tall, black haired man through a blue smoke haze.

'What do we know about this man Colter?' he asked.

'Not a great deal, Colonel,' Royce admitted with a sense of frustration. 'All I've heard is talk. He sells guns. Spends a great deal of his time in Europe and Latin America.'

'He could be useful to us, Royce.' St Clair stood up. He was a tall man, broad in the shoulders, but held himself ramrod straight. His posture was a reminder of his military background. 'When he arrives with that Debenham girl I'll sound him out.'

'Do you want him watched, sir?'

St Clair's smile was without humour. 'Of course, Royce. The girl too. But do it with discretion. If Colter is genuine I do not want him offended. On the other hand we do have to look out for our own safety. I'll leave it in your hands.'

'You can do that, Colonel.'

St Clair knew he could. Royce was an ideal second in command. He was always one step ahead, possessing an ability to anticipate well. Which was a valuable talent in a fighting man. St Clair watched him leave the room.

God, if I had a few hundred more like Royce things would be different!

St Clair shrugged off the impatience that crowded his mind. Why was he so restless? Maybe because matters were building up to a climax. With the first phase of the operation due to take place very shortly. He was pleased with the way things were going. More recruits joining them. The financial backing still coming in. So why was he so restless?

The matter of the warehouse raid in Galveston kept niggling at the back of his mind. It had happened more than ten days ago, and they had gotton away free and clear. Nothing had come from the death of the US Deputy Royce had killed. It had been a pity Royce had acted so quickly. In retrospect he should have taken him somewhere safe and questioned him. Learned how much the man knew, and whether he had passed any information to his superiors. If one man could learn about their plans so could others. So concern remained in St Clair's mind. Not enough to put a stop to his plans. Nothing could do that. He was not about to be diverted from his purpose at this stage. Only death would do that. No living power could stop him now. Too many years had gone by, and there was far too much of himself in the Brotherhood. It was the force that kept him alive. He fought the battle for a return to the old ways on every level, in all extremes. As a duly elected Senator he fought willingly for anything that would benefit the South, and opposed any motion that might bring her harm. He was not a popular man. That didn't worry him in the slightest.

St Clair stood before one of the room's huge windows, looking out across across the smooth lawns surrounding his Louisiana home. It always gave him a feeling of security and permanency when he surveyed the St Clair property. The great house, the land and the responsibility that went with it, had been in the St Clair family for over one hundred years. It had taken a great deal of effort to rebuild the stature of the estate after the War, but St Clair had done it without a word of complaint. He saw it as his duty, and saw the strengthening of the Brotherhood in the same light. It was something that had to be done. The South — *the Confederacy* — must not be allowed to die. There was too much that was fine and important to be cast aside. St Clair, and many like him, were determined not to let that happen. It was why the Brotherhood was formed. And now it was becoming a force to be reckoned with. When their planned operation came to fruition and doubters in the ranks would be fully convinced.

St Clair smiled to himself. He was proud of the operation. It had been his brainchild from conception to near-completion. He felt elated as he realised how close they were to making it actually happen. When it did the effects would rock Washington to its foundations.

He found his attention drawn to a slim figure crossing the smooth lawn, and the smile left his lips. Why couldn't he feel pride at the sight of his own son? Willard St Clair, the heir to the St Clair legend. Watching his fair haired son's progress across the lawn St Clair could feel nothing but disappointment. Willard had been a failure from the moment of his birth. He had been cursed with a crippled leg that had left him with a limp. St Clair's wife, who had died when the boy had been twelve years old, had coddled and protected him from the harsh realities of life. Even after her death Willard had remained in her shadow. All of St Clair's efforts to toughen the boy had turned sour. All that he saw was Willard turning into a sadistic bully, using his power and influence and wealth to hurt others. In despair St Clair had pushed his feelings towards Parker Royce, using him almost like a substitute son. But he knew he was only fooling himself. There was no way of changing things. They stayed as they were and never became what one wished them to be.

He had no worries over his daughter Lucilla. She was a woman any man would be proud of. Not only beautiful Lucilla possessed a personality capable of adjusting to any situation. She had a fiery spirit and a dedication to her father's cause that knew no limits. St Clair knew that when the man called

Colter arrived, Lucilla would turn on her charms. If he was any kind of a man Colter would find her hard to resist, and under those circumstances Lucilla would soon find out who he really was.

St Clair turned from the window. He had things to do. Arrangements to make for the arrival of Lady Sarah Debenham and Colter. And then he had to supervise the removal of the weapons taken from Galveston and other raids. The weapons lay in the vast cellars under the great house. It was time to move them to the main cache.

The Louisiana Bayou country, in and around Barataria Bay, was excellent for St Clair's purpose. Beyond the boundary of his vast estate the cultivated land gave way almost immediately to miles of swampland, bordered on the East by the Mississippi and the Gulf coast on the South. It was wild, primitive country, dangerous in the extreme to anyone who ventured into it without knowledge of the trackless area. Beauregard St Clair had been born and raised in this country. In his youth he had spent long days in the company of an old Creole hunter. A man who knew the Bayou better than most men knew themselves. He had taught St Clair everything he knew, showing him the safe ground and the secret trails. Places where a hundred men could hide and never be found. St Clair had learned and remembered. That knowledge had provided him with the perfect place to secrete the stolen weapons for the Brotherhood.

Soon those weapons would be put to good use, and a new chapter in Southern history would be written.

In blood and fire.

4

The only knowledge Brand had of the Barataria Bay area was that it had provided a refuge for the Lafitte brothers, Jean and Pierre, back around the 1810–1815 period.

First a pirate sanctuary.

And now?

The question formed itself but remained unanswered, and would stay that way until his investigation got under way.

The trip from Galveston to New Orleans had been long. The final stage had seemed even longer, despite the comfortable coach provided by Beauregard St Clair. Brand ached in every joint. Dust sifted up through the floorboards as the coach bounced and swayed along the trail. Brand felt sweaty and irritable.

He glanced at Sarah, wondering how she managed to remain so cool and relaxed. She smiled at his scowl.

'Beautiful country,' she said conversationally.

Brand muttered something she didn't catch. She sensed his sour mood and laughed. She moved to his side and leaned close to him, the cool scent of her perfume invading his nostrils.

'Hey, remember me?'

She didn't give him time to answer. Her soft mouth closed over his. For a while there was silence. And then the coach hit a deep rut, lurching violently. Sarah gasped as the roll of the coach pushed her into the far corner.

'Maybe we should wait until we're on firmer ground,' she suggested.

Brand leaned across to pull her close.

'To hell with waiting,' he growled.

'Jason, I'm going to miss you,' she said out of the blue.

He stared at her. 'What brought that on?'

'You'll get the feel for your work again,' she said wistfully, touching his cheek. 'Once that happens I won't stand a chance.'

Brand had no answer. Because deep down he knew she was right. He was already thinking ahead, planning his initial moves once they reached the St Clair residence.

'You see,' Sarah said. 'I'm already losing you.'

They completed the rest of the journey in a restless silence. Brand wanted to reassure her — *but reassure about what?* That she was right? That her feelings spoke the truth? He felt a momentary stab of guilt, then pushed the thoughts aside. Hadn't he made it clear from the start how things would be? She had appeared to have understood and accepted the situation. Maybe they had both been fooling each other, and let things go too far. Brand stared out of the coach window, watching the blue sky slash by through the dense greenery that fringed the road. In contrast his mood was dark and brooding.

The St Clair estate was reached in

early evening. The flat fields of cotton began to appear. As they rolled on through the lush countryside Brand spotted various buildings dotted around the estate in close proximity to the great house itself. He wondered if any of them held anything of interest. There was only one way to find out.

The coach swept around a curving, gravelled drive and came to rest before the high doors of the sprawling mansion.

A Negro in maroon livery opened the door and helped Sarah to step down. Brand followed, grateful to be stretching his legs. As he took a deep breath he caught the heavy scent of blossom. The rich fragrance seemed to cling to him.

The Negro led them into the house. A couple more servants appeared and followed them inside with their luggage. They moved into the huge entrance hall. On the far side a wide staircase led to the upper floor. Glittering chandeliers had already been lit against the approaching darkness.

'*Welcome! Welcome!*'

The voice that boomed across the hall could not have been anything but Southern. Brand glanced in its direction and found himself face to face with Beauregard St Clair. Tall and powerfully built, with a mane of fair hair, St Clair was an impressive figure. From the file McCord had shown him, Brand recalled that the man was in his late forties. He didn't look it. He moved easily, lightly, and carried himself with the ease of a much younger man. St Clair crossed the hall, a smile on his handsome face. In front of Sarah he bowed from the waist.

'Lady Sarah, you honour this house with your presence. Lucilla will be down in a moment. She returned late from riding. I hope you can forgive this tardiness.'

'Nothing to forgive, Senator.' Sarah smiled graciously. She held out a hand in Brand's direction. 'May I introduce Mister Peter Colter.'

'You are most welcome, sir.'

Brand took the outstretched hand. He felt the latent power of the fingers that gripped his, and when he met St Clair's gaze he knew he was being sized up. The Senator's bored into Brand's, and they were the coldest eyes Brand head ever seen.

'I've heard a great deal about you, Senator.'

St Clair laughed. A genuinely warm sound. 'And none of it good I dare say.'

'At least it means they're paying attention to you.'

St Clair was still smiling.

'I expect you good people could do with a chance to freshen up.' The Senator gestured to one of the Negro servants. 'Frederick, show our guests to their rooms. Dinner will be in an hour. I'll see you then. If you will excuse me for the moment. I have things to attend to.'

St Clair turned and left them. Brand and Sarah followed the Negro up the stairs. They were on the first landing when a figure appeared before them.

'Oh, Sarah, how can you ever forgive me!'

The accent was delightful. The owner was beautiful. A genuine daughter of the South, Brand decided. This was Lucilla St Clair. Brand's gaze lingered on the slim but womanly body under the crisp white blouse and dark skirt. The hair that fell below the slender shoulders was as fine as silk and the colour of spun gold. Brilliant, startlingly blue eyes focussed on Brand, the soft pink lips forming into a faint, inquiring smile.

'I'm sure you could be forgiven anything, Miss St Clair. Anything at all.'

Lucilla's smile widened. 'I do like your friend, Sarah.'

Sarah gave Brand a sideways glance that almost had physical impact, and he realised she was showing signs of jealousy. When she spoke she concealed her feelings.

'Oh, everyone likes him,' she said. 'He has such a way with people. And it's good to see you again, Lucilla.

Thank you for the invite.'

'You don't realise how good it is to have some fresh faces around this place. It does get a little lonely out here. Being so far from New Orleans doesn't help.'

'It is rather a long journey,' Sarah agreed.

'Shame on me,' Lucilla gushed. 'Here I am chattering away and you poor things must be dying to freshen up.'

Lucilla radiated charm as if it was sunshine, Brand realised, but underneath he suspected she was as tough as old hickory.

Shortly after Brand was closing the door of his room. He tossed his hat on the bed, stripped off his jacket and black tie, opening his shirt collar. Crossing the room he opened the louvered doors that allowed access to the balcony outside. It was rimmed by wrought iron railings. The darkness was falling fast now and a faint breeze drifted across the wide lawns flanking the house. Brand stayed on the balcony for a while. He was about to go back inside when he caught sight of a figure moving along the path at the east end of the house. It was the way the man moved that held Brand's attention. He wasn't out for an evening stroll. The man moved with a definite purpose, head turning right to left and back again as he checked the area. And he was carrying a rifle. The man was on patrol. He was a guard. An armed guard at that.

Brand watched the man a while longer. His curiosity was well aroused by what he had seen. Just what was so important it needed armed guards to keep it secure?

He was brought back into the room by a tap on the door that led to the attached bathroom. Brand opened the door and was confronted by the Negro servant Frederick.

'Your bath is ready, sir.'

'Thank you, Frederick.'

The bathroom was tiled and sumptuous. The water hot and scented. Brand stripped off his dusty clothing and lowered himself into the water. He wondered if Sarah was doing the same and decided his bathing would have been more enjoyable if she'd been with him. He found himself smiling at her reaction to his response to Lucilla St Clair. She must have expected some kind of reaction. Lucilla was the kind of woman who could have made a ninety-year-old man sit up and take notice. And Jason Brand was a long way off ninety.

He soaked for a good half hour. When he returned to his room, wrapped in a huge towel, he found that his luggage had been opened and his evening suit laid out on the bed. The white shirt with the frilled front, that Sarah had chosen for him was there, along with underclothes and socks. His boots had been polished until they gleamed.

Brand dressed leisurely. When he had finished he picked up the attache case beside the bed. Unlocking it with the key on his watch chain he laid it on the bed, raising the lid. He took out his big .45 calibre Colt. Next he removed the Colt-special that Whitfield, the armourer had adapted for him. He had carried the weapon for the first time during the assignment that had taken him to Miles City, where he had met Sarah. The conclusion of that assignment had left Brand near death at the hands of the man named Raven. Brand checked that both weapons were fully loaded, then returned them to the case and locked it again.

When he made his way downstairs and was crossing the hall, Lucilla appeared. She had changed too. The blouse and skirt were gone, replaced by a slim fitting black dress that left little to the imagination. Her hair was piled on top of her head and a diamond pendant, suspended from a thin sliver chain, lay in the deep cleft between her full breasts.

'Now you do look better,' she said teasingly.

Brand took her offered arm and

Lucilla led him to the dining room. Sarah was already seated at the long table. At its head sat Beauregard St Clair. There were two other men at the table. St Clair introduced them.

'My son Willard.' The slender, blonde young man nodded briefly in Brand's direction, looking away quickly. 'And this is Parker Royce, my estate manager amongst other things.'

'They tell me you're something of an authority on guns, Mister Colter,' Royce said evenly.

Brand sat down, glancing across at Royce. The man was smiling, but there was a hardness behind the outer mask. Royce had the look of a killer about him. There was controlled violence just below the surface.

'Dare say I could work out one end from the other.'

Royce's eyes glittered in the moment before he turned aside and said something to Sarah that brought a smile to her lips.

St Clair was a good host. The meal

was an experience. They started with Green Turtle soup, followed by fresh salmon and green salad. There was choice of wild turkey or stuffed roast quail. Brand lost count of the accompanying dishes of vegetables and sauces. He ate sparingly, having learned long ago that heavy meals didn't go together with the hectic requirements of his work.

Later the men retired to St Clair's booklined study, leaving Lucilla and Sarah on their own. In the study the Senator produced fine brandy and cigars.

'I'd hazard a guess that you find numerous markets for your weapons in Europe and Latin America, Mister Colter,' he ventured.

'There always seems to be something going on somewhere,' Brand replied.

'Does it pay well?' Royce asked bluntly.

Brand looked at him through a wreath of cigar smoke. 'I won't starve, Mr Royce.'

'And where do you get your weapons from, Colter?' Willard St Clair asked.

Brand eyes St Clair's son. It had been a clumsy question, badly framed. From what he had seen of the man Brand judged Willard to be spoiled and with a sullen attitude. He didn't like the young man very much.

'Please don't embarrass our guest,' St Clair butted in quickly, frowning at his son.

'I have my sources of supply,' Brand said. 'And like any good businessman I protect them.'

'Of course, of course,' Beauregard St Clair agreed. 'I'd expect nothing less.'

From then on St Clair steered the conversation along mundane lines. There was no more mention of guns, but Brand had the feeling the matter would eventually be broached once more.

Parker Royce glanced at his watch some time later. He drained his brandy glass and stood up.

'If you will excuse me, gentleman. I have things to attend to.'

St Clair nodded. 'Go ahead, Parker.'

'Busy man,' Brand said as Royce left the study.

'I couldn't ask for better. Nothing that boy can't turn his hand to.'

Brand tended to agree with that. He decided that Parker Royce would turn out to have a great deal of hidden talents.

'More brandy, Mister Colter?'

Brand shook his head. 'If you don't mind, Senator, I'd like to retire. It's been a long day.'

'Of course, my boy, how thoughtless of me. Perhaps a ride before breakfast?'

'That would be my pleasure, sir.'

He crossed the hall and made his way upstairs. The landing lay in deep shadow, the darkness broken by the soft glow of oil lamps. Brand reached his room without seeing anyone. He wondered if Sarah had already gone to bed.

Inside his room he changed into black pants and shirt. Settling down on the bed he lit a cigar and sat back to wait until the rest of the house retired for the night.

5

Brand closed the cover of his watch and returned it to the pocket of his coat draped over the back of a chair. It was well after two o'clock. He stood up and crossed the bedroom to lock the door. From the small bedside table he picked up the .45 calibre Colt and tucked it under his belt. Turning, he opened the doors and stepped out onto the balcony. The warm musk of the Louisiana night reached out to envelope him. He could hear the subdued racket of insects drifting out of the darkness. Brand stood for a while, allowing his eyes to become adjusted to the gloom. Luckily there was a pale moon overhead; he decided it could be just as much of a hazard as a help.

He waited for the guard he'd seen earlier. The man appeared a minute or so later, still pacing the same route.

Brand wasn't sure if it was actually the same man. If it was he had a hell of a constitution. Brand studied the man's route for a while, working out his timing. At the furthest point of his route it took the man just over three minutes before he returned. It wasn't long but Brand figured it would give him enough time to get down to ground level from the balcony.

The moment the guard turned on his return trek Brand readied himself. As the dark figure walked out of view Brand swung himself over the balcony rail and started down. The St Clair mansion had been constructed from rough-hewn stone that provided plenty of hand and footholds. Even so it took Brand a good two minutes to reach the ground, and he was sweating by the time the descent was over. He also had a few skinned fingertips.

Brand eased the Colt from his belt. He pressed in close to the wall and ran towards the east wing of the mansion. The guard seemed to be concentrating his attention on that part of the building. Brand decided it would be as well to start looking there.

He was almost at the far end of the wall when the guard re-appeared. There was no chance to avoid a confrontation. The guard opened his mouth to yell, turning towards Brand's lunging figure. The rifle flashed in the moonlight as it slashed at Brand's body. Still moving forward Brand slapped it aside with his left arm, and by some stroke of luck it didn't go off. Driving in close Brand slammed the barrel of his Colt into the guard's face. He felt the solid impact. Heard the guard's choked off cry. The man stumbled backwards, slumping against the wall, his face washed with a sudden rush of blood. Brand hit him again, this time across the skull, and the guard flopped to the ground.

Turning away Brand rounded the end of the mansion. He was breathing hard, angry too that trouble had reared its head so early in the game. He knew there was no use worrying over the incident. He was here to do a job, and no one had ever said it was going to be easy. The sooner he moved into his assignment the better he would like it. Playing *Colter* made him uncomfortable.

The moment he rounded the corner he found what he was looking for. A shallow ramp that led down to a pair of low wooden doors. A cellar entrance. A likely place to hide a consignment of stolen weapons. *Maybe too likely,* he found himself thinking. He could imagine Beauregard St Clair having a little more cunning than that. There was a chance that this was nothing more than a temporary cache. Just a holding place before they were moved to a secure hideaway. Brand decided he was wasting time debating the point. There was only one way to find out.

The thick, studded doors were secured by heavy chains and a padlock. Brand saw that the lock was fairly new and well oiled. The earth on the ramp bore deep rut marks of the kind left by a heavy-laden wagon. The cellar was frequently used for something.

An impulse sent Brand to where the unconscious guard lay. The man showed no signs of recovering yet. Brand searched the man's pockets and found what he was looking for.

A key.

When Brand tried it in the lock it worked. Brand eased open the doors and slipped inside, pulling the door shut behind him. He found himself in total darkness, and somewhere off in the distance he heard a sound that caused the hairs to stand up on the back of his neck.

Soft scratching sounds accompanied by shrill squeaking.

Rats!

He didn't like the creatures. Knew few people who did. He would have rather faced a man with a loaded gun than a rat in a dark cellar.

Gradually his eyes adjusted to the gloom and he began to make out dark shapes. Now he could see a rectangle of light and realised it was a small barred window. He began to move deeper into the cellar. The air was stale. Dusty but holding a touch of dampness. It made him think of the swampland that lay beyond the St Clair estate.

At regular intervals thick stone pillars rose from the floor to the low ceiling. They seemed to be supporting the very structure of the mansion itself. Brand wondered how far under the house the cellar extended.

He spotted a dark shape against one crumbling, mildewed wall. A heavy waterproof canvas lay over the shape. Tucking the Colt behind his belt Brand dragged the canvas clear. Even in the dim light he was able to identify the long wooden boxes that were stacked under the canvas. He recalled the list McCord had itemised. They were all here. The cased Gatling guns. Rifles. The Colt revolvers. Boxes of ammunition. He recovered the boxes.

A feeling of unease crept over Brand. He had found part of what he was looking for. Maybe he had found it too easily. Brand always figured if things went too well early in the assignment there was a hard fall waiting somewhere ahead. *Damn*, he thought. *Maybe he was getting soft. Came with being off the job for too long.*

He barely picked up the whisper of sound behind him. It was close. Just to his right. Brand leaned forward and to the left, twisting as he moved. He caught a glimpse of a tawny face in the light of a flickering torch. Broad nostrils flaring in anger above a thick lipped mouth. Tight curled mid-brown hair over a strong skull.

A Mulatto.

There was no more time for observation. The Mulatto, naked to the waist, lunged at Brand, the torch he was carrying thrust at his face. Brand felt the sting of heat dry the sweat on his flesh. He pulled away from the fire, slamming against the crates at his back. He couldn't move further. There was only one way to go — so he took it. He kicked out, the toe of his boot catching the Mulatto across one knee. The blow was hard, drawing a gasp of pain from the man's lips. He paused in mid-stride, giving Brand the opportunity to push away from the stacked crates and carry his attack forward. He ducked under the lash of the blazing torch, slamming a hard fist into the Mulatto's taut belly. It was like striking a sandbag. The man had muscles like ridged iron. Brand hit him again, a third time. This time the Mulatto retreated a few steps. Then a knee came out of nowhere and smashed into Brand's hip, spinning him back. Numbness caused him to stumble, go down on his knees. Throwing a quick glance in the Mulatto's direction he saw the grinning man coming at him again. Brand clawed for the Colt tucked in his belt.

It wasn't there!

The blazing torch was pushed at him again. Brand tried to pull away from the curling tongues of flame. He only partially avoided it. The tip of the torch caught his left shoulder, burning through the thin material of his shirt, searing the flesh. Brand gasped against the sudden pain. In desperation he let himself sink to the floor, under the Mulatto's reach, hands clawing at the cellar floor for a weapon. Anything. His fingers located a chunk of crumbling stone. A fist-sized lump of loose masonry. Brand closed his fingers around the stone, looked up to see the Mulatto bending towards him. The man was still grinning, triumph in his eyes reflected in the glow of the torch. He was about to jab the torch at Brand's face. Brand thrust up off the floor, swinging the chunk of stone at the grinning face. It struck with a sodden thud. Something crunched and the Mulatto's face was suddenly wet with blood. A yell of pained surprise bubbled from his mashed lips. He dropped the torch and clutched at his ruined face. Brand drove up off the floor, going for the man in a savage rush. He clubbed him across the side of the head with the stone, then dropped it and used his fists. His telling blows knocked the Mulatto off balance. The man stumbled drunkenly, falling against the stacked crates. He hung there for long seconds until Brand's powerful blows drove him to the cellar floor.

Brand snatched up the torch. Casting around he located his dropped Colt. He knew he had to get out of the cellar before anyone else showed up. He was angry at the way things were going because he was breaking his cover with every step he was taking.

He turned back towards the door he'd entered by, and was in time to see it swing open. Dark figures rushed into the cellar. The door was blocked as his way of escape. Brand turned aside, moving deeper into the cellar.

A gun fired behind him. The shot was loud in the confines of the cellar. The bullet slammed into a stone pillar. Crumbling stone spewed in a dusty shower. More shots followed, seeking Brand as he kept on moving. He could feel their passing through the darkness around him. He reached another of the stone pillars and put it between himself and the gunmen. Bullets slammed into the stone with deadly force. Brand suddenly realised he was still carrying the blazing torch. Swearing at his own stupidity he threw the torch as far away from him as he could. It landed yards away, still burning, and casting a wavering light out of the darkness.

Brand listened. It had gone quiet. His pursuers were still back there, in the shadows. Waiting. They wanted him to show himself. To give them a target. Brand had no intention of doing that. There was no way he was going to let himself be shot down out of hand. If they wanted to play a waiting game he was willing. It wouldn't be the first time he'd done it, and he had the patience of an Apache when it came to this kind of thing.

The time stretched. Long, silent minutes.

Then Brand heard a faint sound off

to his right. He glanced in the direction of the noise, pinpointing the spot. At first there was nothing. Then he saw a vague shape moving just beyond the glow of the discarded torch. The shape realised itself into a man with a raised handgun. He was edging round to Brand's side of the pillar.

Lifting the big Colt Brand braced the weapon with his left hand, tracking the moving man. He held his target for a moment, gently stroking the trigger and the moment the gun fired, he cocked and fired a second bullet. He saw the man fall. Heard a low moan.

'Hey, Ed! Ed, you hurt?'

Brand moved quickly and fired at the sound of the voice. A man cursed in a hurt tone. A hunched figure stumbled into the pale rectangle of the open doorway. Brand fired at it, his bullet tearing a chunk of wood from the surround.

Breaking cover Brand raced for the open door. He had to get out fast. Before more of them came. There was a chance they didn't know who the intruder was. Maybe he could make it back to his room before they spotted him. He didn't give it much hope, but it was at least worth a try.

He went through the door on the run, keeping low. Up the ramp and then angling for the corner of the building.

He almost made it. Then a gunshot split the night. Sharp chips of stone stung his face. Brand stumbled forward, anger and frustration fuelling his movements. He had made a bad start, and if he wasn't careful matters weren't about to get much better.

He heard voices now, shouting back and forth. There were more of them than he'd realised. A new sound added itself to the general din. The vicious growling bark of dogs. They were going to set the damn hounds on him.

A bitter chuckle forced itself from his lips. He'd been yearning for a return to action. For something more stimulating than waiting around cooling his heels. The way things were going he was certain to get more than his share.

He rounded the end of the house. It seemed an eternity before he reached the spot below his balcony. Brand jammed the Colt behind his belt. He placed his hands against the wall, ready to start climbing.

A voice reached him out of the shadows.

'Just keep them there! The Colonel's going to want you alive. For now at least.'

Brand heard soft footsteps behind him. The muzzle of a gun ground into his spine. A hand snatched his Colt from his belt.

'You've been having a busy night, Mister Colter.'

'I needed the exercise after that meal, Royce.'

Parker Royce laughed dryly.

'Turn around, Colter. But keep those hands where I can see them.'

As Brand faced about he saw other figures moving up to crowd around Royce. Flickering torches cast long, wavering shadows. Brand glanced at Royce. The man was studying him intently, as if he was trying to strip away the mask and see the real Brand.

'I'd kill you here and now if there weren't answers I need from you. Better believe that, Colter.'

'I always believe everything I'm told when a man has a gun on me.'

'This bastard thinks he's funny,' one of the men behind Brand said.

'We'll give him something to laugh over soon enough,' Royce snapped. 'Charly, take the boys and have a look round the cellar. Find out what he's been up to and let me know.'

The men drifted away, leaving Brand and Royce alone.

'Move out. The Colonel doesn't like being kept waiting.'

Brand didn't give a damn what the Colonel did or didn't like. But he walked ahead of Royce, fully aware of the cocked gun nudging his spine. There was no percentage in arguing with those odds.

Royce took him into St Clair's booklined study and closed the door behind them.

Beauregard St Clair was standing before a log fire burning in the massive stone hearth. He was fully dressed, as immaculate as he had been earlier in the evening. Only his manner had changed. The courteous host had vanished. Now Brand faced a dangerously aroused fanatic. St Clair's eyes were fixed on Brand's face and never wavered for a moment.

'You have disappointed me, Mister Colter. And you have insulted my hospitality. You were welcomed as a guest in my house and repay me by acting like a common thief.'

'You speaking as a US Senator now, or as a big wheel in the Brotherhood?'

Brand felt a surge of satisfaction at St Clair's reaction.

'I won't waste time denying it,' he replied after composing himself. 'As you will not be leaving here alive there's no reason to maintain any pretence.

The Brotherhood exists. It's getting stronger all the time. Very shortly we'll be ready to make our presence known.' He jabbed a finger in Brand's direction. *'Do you really think you could stop us?'*

Brand allowed a thin smile to curl his mouth.

'We stopped you last time,' he said softly.

'Bastard!'

The word exploded from Parker Royce's lips. He slammed the barrel of his pistol down across the back of Brand's skull, driving him to his knees.

'A fitting place for Yankee scum,' St Clair said.

'Colonel, we need to know who sent him,' Royce insisted. 'How much information does he have on us and the Brotherhood.'

St Clair nodded.

'You're right, Parker. This is the second time someone has got too close for comfort. But this time we get answers. Make this man talk before you kill him.'

'Colonel, what about the woman?'

St Clair glanced down at Brand, then across at Royce.

'Keep her locked in her room until we've dealt with this one. Time to investigate her later.' Concentration clouded St Clair's features. 'Parker, we need to work out some emergency measures. Let us assume the worst. That we are not as secure as we believed. Too much can go wrong for us at this stage if we're not careful. But deal with this Yankee spy first. Get him out of my sight. Cut him into little chunks if you have to, but make him talk.'

St Clair strode out of the room, slamming the door behind him.

Brand raised his aching head and stared into Parker Royce's hard face. The gun in the man's hand had taken on the aspect of a cannon.

'I'm going to enjoy this,' Royce said, and Brand had a feeling he would do well to believe what the man was saying. 'On your feet and don't do a damn thing out of place.'

They left the study and passed through the deserted hall. Down a narrow side passage with a single door at the far end. Beyond the door was a small bare room. The only furniture in the room was a table and a couple of wooden chairs.

'Sit down, Colter,' Royce said, indicating one of the chairs with the ever-present gun. 'Make the most of it. I won't tell you to get comfortable.'

Brand sat down. He didn't even try to imagine what was about to happen. His mind was already beyond that. It was working on a way to get him out of the clutches of the Brotherhood. He kept his eye on Royce at the same time, trying to judge the man's potential. It didn't take him long to realise he'd have to move fast to catch the man off guard. For some reason an image of Sarah came into his mind. He hoped she was unharmed. *If the bastards touched her!* His anger evaporated. There wasn't a deal he could do for her until he got himself out of trouble.

The door opened. A squat, broad man shuffled in. He had dark skin and his head was completely bald. A great jagged scar ran across one side of his naked skull and down the side of his face to the jawline. Following close behind this man was a figure Brand couldn't fail to recognise. It was the Mulatto he'd fought with in the cellar. The Mulatto's face was a bloody ruin. The stone Brand had hit him with had crushed one side of his face, closing one eye and tearing a raw gash in his flesh.

'I believe you already met Rico,' Royce said with relish. He indicated the man with the scar. 'This is Mantee. He's a specialist. He likes to hurt people and he's damn good at it.'

Mantee grinned. His teeth were large and yellow and crooked. He held up a pair of huge, scarred hands and closed them into even larger fists.

'St Clair tell you our little problem?' Royce asked and Mantee nodded. He was still nodding when, without warning, he turned and punched Brand in the face. The blow was heavy and the impact slammed Brand out of the chair, dumping him brutally on the stone floor. He lay on his face, stunned and gasping for breath. The side of his face that had taken the blow was numb. Blood flowed from his mouth where he had bitten his tongue. Before he could move the Mulatto, Rico stepped forward. He dragged Brand to his feet and slammed him bodily against the wall. Brand grunted. He caught a glimpse of Mantee coming towards him. Brand tried to pull away but Rico had him secured. Mantee's great fists drove in at Brand's body and face. Over and over. The blows rocked Brand's body, pain surging with every punch. He lashed out wildly, managing to land a couple of blows of his own, though they failed to have any effect on Mantee. A crippling punch caught Brand across the side of the head, tearing him out of Rico's hands. He slithered helplessly along the rough wall, falling to his knees. A knee in the side drove him to the floor where he lay coughing and spitting blood. Through dazed eyes he saw Mantee and Rico looming over him, their blows raining down on him in a torrent. Then a pause, and blinking his eyes against the haze Brand saw Parker Royce leaning over him.

'Enough?' Royce asked conversationally. 'Maybe you feel like talking now?'

They hauled him to the chair and let him slump forward. Royce sat on the edge of the table and waited until Brand had recovered enough to be able to acknowledge him.

'Time for real names,' Royce suggested. 'Colter isn't your name. So who are you?'

Brand lifted his battered, bloody head, even managing a pained smile.

'*Go to hell.*'

Royce shook his head. 'Wrong answer, friend.' He sighed. 'Maybe it's time to bring in the little lady. I figure five minutes with Mantee should have her talking.'

'Touch her, Royce, and I'll see you dead. Even if I have to crawl out my grave to do it.'

Mantee laughed harshly. He stood in front of Brand.

'Let me bring her down here. Let him *see*.'

Royce considered. 'Could be the way. Go fetch her, Mantee.'

The words registered in Brand's dulled mind. Mantee was leaving the room. That left two. Still heavy odds in his condition but most likely the best hand he was going to get in this game.

Parker Royce smiled in Brand's direction. 'Could have saved you some pain if I'd thought of this earlier.'

Lyin' son of a bitch, Brand thought. *You enjoyed every damn minute of it.*

Royce, still grinning, glanced across at the Mulatto.

'A white woman for you, Rico. All for yourself.'

Brand launched himself out of the

chair, hands reaching for the gun Royce was holding. He struck the Southerner and they both fell back across the table. As they rolled to the far side the table tilted and threw them to the stone floor. Royce landed first, a pained grunt bursting from his lips as his head cracked against the hard floor. Brand jerked the gun from his fingers, turned it and lashed out. The barrel smacked up against Royce's jaw, opening a bloody gash. Twisting his body Brand rolled across the floor until he was brought to a halt by the far wall. He pushed himself into a sitting position, head turning as Rico lunged across the room at him, growling his rage. Rico had pulled a wicked knife from his belt. Brand didn't even think about it. He simply lifted the gun he'd taken from Royce and fired twice. Two swift shots that hammered into Rico's chest, turning him aside and spilling him to his knees. The howling Mulatto went down hard, his blood bubbling out across the stone floor.

Brand shoved to his feet, fighting off the lethargy that was threatening to hold him back. He flung open the door and staggered into the passage. He used the wall to keep him upright. The end of the passage seemed a mile away. When he reached the hall he made a run for the stairs. The only image in his mind was of Mantee and Sarah. He summoned some hidden reserve and went up the stairs in a loping run.

He reached the first landing and heard Sarah scream. The sound of heavy footsteps. Then she called his name as a warning.

He saw movement ahead of him. Then the crash of a shot. The bullet ripped a long sliver of wood out of the bannister. A second shot rattled its echo across the landing.

Brand dropped to the floor.

He heard the thump of boots.

Getting louder.

A shadow fell across the floor ahead of him, followed by a third shot.

This one came too close.

Brand returned fire. Two close shots, placed with the inbuilt accuracy that had kept him alive too many times in the past.

A man grunted. The noise became a wet gurgle. Mantee stepped into view, looking in Brand's direction but not seeing him. The front of his shirt was red with blood. His mouth dribbled more. He paused as his limbs lost their coordination and then tumbled face down on the landing.

Brand climbed to his feet.

'*Sarah!*'

'I'm here.'

He saw her as she moved out of a doorway. She wore a thin nightdress that had been almost ripped from her body. Brand didn't say anything. He took her hand and hurried her to the door of his room. The door was still locked from the inside. Brand used his boot to kick it open. He pushed Sarah into the room and went directly for his attache case. He took out the Colt Special and jammed it under his belt.

He located a box of .45 calibre shells. Tipping them out he scooped up a handful and jammed the cartridges into his pocket.

'Jason, what's going on?' Sarah demanded. Her tone speared through his jumbled thoughts.

'Just get that nightdress off,' he snapped, crossing the room to where his case of clothes stood at the foot of the bed.

'*What?*'

He spilled clothes onto the bed.

'Either put something on, or go like you are.'

She realised what he wanted her to do. While she dressed Brand kept watch at the door. He knew they were short on time. Somehow they had to get out of the house. Outside they might have a chance.

'Sarah, get a move on. This isn't a damn social evening we're going to.'

Her snapped reply surprised him. He hadn't realised she knew such colourful language.

Moments later she was by his side.

'So, are we going to stand here all night?' she asked.

As they left the room Brand heard voices coming from downstairs. That way was barred to them. Brand decided that a house of this size must have a number of exits, he took Sarah's hand and pulled her behind him as they moved along the passage. At its end Brand noticed a narrow side passage. They moved along it and found a flight of unlit stairs. They went down. The stairs were steep and seemed to go on forever. At the bottom was a locked door. Brand didn't hesitate. He used his boot to pummel the door until it burst open. A familiar smell reached his nostrils from the chill darkness beyond. The damp, mildew stench of the cellars.

'God, do we have to go in there?' Sarah asked.

'Yeah.'

He took her hand, pulling her close behind as he advanced into the cellar.

He was certain they were going in the right direction.

Ahead of them sound and light emerged from the gloom. Brand pushed Sarah up behind one of the great pillars. He pressed the Colt special into her hand. Her eyes were wide with alarm as she looked at him. Brand thumbed fresh shells into the gun he'd taken from Royce.

'Stay here,' he told her. 'I want to see what's going on up there. I'll be back.'

Moving from pillar to pillar Brand approached the activity. He was finally able to stand and watch a half-dozen men loading the stolen arms cache onto a flatbed wagon. The ammunition boxes were also being stacked beside the crates of guns. It seemed his intrusion had started something, and he wondered where they were moving the arms to. Had his original guess been correct — that there was another hiding place for the guns? It was certainly starting to look that way.

He returned to where Sarah waited.

'Well?' she asked.

He told her what he had seen. She listened in silence and it suddenly dawned on Brand that she was in the dark concerning Beauregard St Clair's involvement with the Brotherhood. He was going to have to tell her about it, but now wasn't the time or place.

'Sarah, you'll have to trust me for now. Like it or not I've got us involved in a dangerous game. It's what I was sent here for. I didn't mean to drag you in this far but there's no other choice now. You've asked about my work often enough. Looks like you're going to get your answers the hard way.'

Taking her hand again he led her towards the place where the wagon stood. The loading was almost complete. As they watched a canvas was dragged over the flatbed and tied down. Two of the men climbed onto the wagon seat and the team was slapped into motion. The wagon rolled across the cellar and out the open door. The other men followed, not bothering to close the heavy doors behind them.

'Let's go,' Brand said. He led Sarah to the door. From there they were able to watch the wagon moving slowly away from the house. The four men who had followed it outside now climbed on waiting horses and fell in behind the wagon.

'Where do you think they're going?' Sarah asked. 'And what's in the wagon?'

'Stolen weapons and ammunition,' Brand explained. 'And I'd make a guess they're heading for the bayou. Enough places out there to hide a million crates of guns.'

She tugged at his arm. 'Is this what it's all about, Jason? Gun running?'

'I wish it was as simple. Those guns will be used for starting what might turn out to be the second Civil War.'

'Are you serious?'

'Damn right I am, Sarah. Our host of the evening, Senator Beauregard St Clair heads an organisation calling itself The Brotherhood of the Confederacy. They have a very simple agenda. To return the South to the way it was before the War, even if it means starting another one to achieve it.'

'That's foolish, Jason. It just couldn't be done.'

'Try telling that to St Clair and his followers. They figure they have it all worked out. They have the men. The influence and the money. And they're stockpiling weapons.'

'It's a nightmare.' Sarah stared at him, eyes registering her shock. 'But what can you do? One man against all those? Good lord, Jason, you look as if you've run over by a herd of cattle already.'

He smiled. 'That's what it feels like.'

Brand realised they had been static for too long. He pointed to a stand of trees on the far side of the sweeping lawn.

'Stay close and keep moving. Doesn't matter what you hear. Don't stop until we're under cover.'

They eased away from the shadows of the house. Once they were out in the open, crossing the smooth, flat lawn, it felt as if the eyes of the world were on them. Nothing happened. They reached the trees without incident, dropping to the ground to regain their breath.

'God, Jason, how long do we have to keep this up?'

'Only until we find out where they're taking those guns.'

Sarah sighed with resignation.

'Serves me right for asking!'

6

Beauregard St Clair's rage was overwhelming. He could hardly believe that both the man known as Colter and the girl had gone. He lost control for a time, raging about the house in a blind fury. Too much was at stake to let anything happen now. His mind worked furiously. He realised he needed to think clearly. To plan ahead. And gradually his anger subsided, leaving him cold and back in control. He returned to his study and called for Parker Royce.

'Well?'

Royce stood before him, humiliation showing on his face. There was a great open gash across the left side of his jaw. St Clair decided that Royce's mental hurt pained him more than the physical wound.

'They've gone into the bayou. We

picked up their tracks but lost them once they reached the swamp.'

'He'll be following the wagon,' St Clair said. 'Trying to find the cache. He's made his mistake, Parker. The bayous run for miles. A stranger will wander round them forever.' He smiled. 'We might not need to waste any bullets on them. The swamp will kill them for us. But let's be sure. Send in the dogs. I want to be certain they don't fall lucky. If Colter finds the cache and by some chance gets away . . . I don't think I have to spell it out for you.'

'No, Colonel,' Royce said. He turned to leave, then hesitated and turned back. 'I let you down tonight, Colonel. Saying sorry won't change it, but it won't happen again.'

'We'll say no more about it, Parker. Every man is entitled to one mistake. *But only one!*'

St Clair's words were still echoing around inside Royce's head as he left the house. The men were already assembled and he gave his orders quickly. The hounds were brought from the kennels, baying eagerly as they sensed a hunt ahead. Royce watched the group as they moved away from the house, heading for the dark, primaeval bayou. It lay out beyond the estate like some evil living organism. Royce didn't like the bayou. It terrified him, though he would never have admitted as much to any living person. Whenever he had to enter the shadowed gloom of the swamp he went cold, dreading every step that took him deeper into the place.

As the sound of the departing men faded, the barking of the savage hounds hanging on the chill air, Royce returned to the house. He wanted to tend the wound on his face before he followed the men. His room was at the rear of the house. It was small and sparsely furnished, but it served its needs. Royce didn't set much store by personal possessions. Money and power were not the driving force of his existence.

Reaching his room he stepped inside.

As he turned from closing the door he sensed he was not alone. Royce dropped his hand to the butt of the revolver in his belt.

'You won't need that, Parker.'

By the light of the oil lamp on the dresser Royce picked out the shape of Lucilla St Clair. He relaxed, letting down the hammer of the revolver. He laid it on the dresser, noticing that Lucilla had brought along a bowl of warm water and bandages. Nor did he fail to notice the thin robe she was wearing so casually. Parker Royce had been aware of her close attention for some time, and though he often experienced sexual feelings for her he contained them. He was after all only an employee and it was wise to temper personal desire with a degree of caution.

'You'll have to excuse me, Miss Lucilla. I guess I'm a little edgy. Been a hectic night so far.'

She smiled.

'I'd call that an understatement,

Parker. Shooting. Killing. Now that man and Sarah Debenham are looking for the guns hidden in the bayou. I'd hazard to say it's been a sight more than hectic.'

'I guess you're right, Miss Lucilla.'

'The night isn't over yet, Parker. Now sit down while I clean up your face. And for God's sake stop calling me *Miss Lucilla*. Do it when father's around if you need to. But not when we're alone. Damnit, Parker, I've seen the way you look at me, and it isn't as the lady of the house.'

She moistened clean cotton and gently wiped the gash on his face. Her touch was light, her closeness a pleasure. The perfume she wore filled his nostrils with its fragrance and Royce felt a stirring in his loins. She was right of course. He wanted her. Badly. But there was a barrier between them, keeping him at a distance. Right now it made things difficult. The thin robe she wore clung to her body, telling him in no uncertain terms that she was naked beneath it.

'There,' she said finally. 'You'll live long enough to settle with that Yankee!'

Royce caught her gaze. The tone of her voice surprised him. There was hate there, directed at the man named Colter.

'Do you think Sarah was in league with him?' she asked suddenly. 'I can hardly believe it. A titled English lady consorting with a Yankee gunman. A killer. I would have believed she had more in common with us.'

'I don't know,' Royce said. 'She's your friend.'

'I thought she was.' Lucilla replied. 'Now I'm not so sure.'

She leaned back against the table, deliberately allowing the robe to part and expose her sleek thighs. She stared at him, a playful smile edging her full lips.

'Don't tell me you were bewitched by her, Parker. Not that I blame you. She is beautiful. Wouldn't you agree?'

He leaned toward her.

'No. You're the beauty.' He paused, then added: 'Lucilla.'

'Well, my oh my,' she breathed softly.

She straightened up, easing the robe open and letting it slip from her silky shoulders. She stood before him totally naked. Her flesh was smooth and flawlessly white. Ripe, full breasts stirred with her breathing, dark nipples erect.

'Parker, I do believe the South is about to rise again,' she whispered huskily.

He rose and went to her, drawing her close, aware of her lush softness thrusting against his own surging hardness. He kissed her roughly, hearing her moan as she slid her arms around him.

'No more lonely nights, Parker Royce. For either of us.'

He carried her to his bed and laid her down, then removed his clothes and slid alongside her. Her slender fingers were eager and bold, touching and holding him, encouraging him. Royce's desire gathered and took control and he lost himself in her scented softness. In the closeness of that small room he devoured her with his passion and Lucilla returned that passion with her own.

7

The bayou was another world!

It was like stepping into the distant past when prehistoric man had just learned to stand upright. A place where time seemed to have stood still and threatened to stay that way for eternity. Everything crowded in on its neighbour. Twisted trees and thick vegetation packed together in tangled masses. So thick in places that pushing through was an impossibility. Fern and swamp grass, cypress, oak and aspen grew in dense stands, connected by the heavy vines that looped and coiled over branches and around trunks, snaking along the ground. Spanish moss clung to the trees, hanging in green fronds. The overall impression was of green lushness underlaid by decay. The air was humid. Dampness clinging to everything. Underfoot the ground felt

93

soft. Spongy. In the gloom it was difficult to determine whether a patch of green was solid ground or thick scum floating on the surface of a brackish pool. The whole bayou seemed to be floating on a lake of still water.

Trailing the slow moving wagon and its outriders had been easy at first. Then rain began to fall. Clouds obscured the moon, and it was shortly after that Brand realised they were lost. The distant sound of the wagon and riders vanished in the mist of falling rain. They struggled on for a while, more than once losing the trail and floundering in water. That was when Brand decided it would be wiser to stop and find somewhere to rest and continue when they had some light.

He spotted a huge, gnarled oak, its massive roots rising out of the sodden earth like twisted limbs. They crawled in amongst them, trying to make themselves comfortable despite the chill rain. Sarah pressed close to him, hoping to gain some warmth from his body.

She had barely spoken since they had left the house, following his instructions without comment or protest, and it was this more than anything that caused Brand's regret at having involved her at all. He knew she wouldn't complain — he wished she would. His main concern was that she might get hurt. By now St Clair would have Sarah down as Brand's accomplice. He'd read enough from the man's file to know that St Clair wouldn't hesitate at harming a woman. Brand cursed inwardly. He had made a bad decision bringing Sarah along. At the outset it had seemed the easiest way of getting an invitation to St Clair's home. It had been a decision based on McCord's orders that he wanted the matter clearing up as quickly as possible. It didn't excuse his reasoning.

Brand drew Sarah closer. She pushed against him. Her acceptance of their situation only increased his guilty feelings. After a while Brand felt a taut smile curl his mouth. McCord's instructions had been for discretion to be the watchword. Already violence and death had thrust their way into the game, and Brand had been on the receiving end of some rough treatment.

The problem with McCord was he spent too much time in Washington. Diplomacy wasn't high on the agenda as far as the Brotherhood was concerned. They only understood one thing. Direct action.

He shivered. It seemed to be getting colder. The rain was heavier. They were already soaked and muddy, but by now beyond caring. Sarah wrapped her arms around him, head down on his chest. Her steady breathing told Brand she was asleep.

The dawn was a long time coming. Brand dozed fitfully. He tried to stay alert in case any of St Clair's men happened on them. The only good thing about the rain was the fact that it would wash away the tracks left by Brand and Sarah. It would make tracking them that much harder.

In the early hours he heard the distant baying of hounds. St Clair had his men and dogs looking for them. The sounds faded. The only consolation was that St Clair's men would be wet and cold too.

Brand watched the grey dawn breaking over the green canopy of the bayou. The rain slackened off as the darkness faded. Beside him Sarah still slept. He eased her aside and climbed to his feet, stiff and aching, eyes bleary. He was still feeling the effects of the beating he'd taken the previous night. Moving into the open he spent fruitless minutes trying to locate their position. It was impossible. There was no point of contact. The bayou looked the same in every direction. He just had no idea where they were, and felt damned foolish about it. Drop him in the middle of the New Mexico badlands and he'd locate himself without even trying. Out here in this green hellhole he was *lost*.

He went back to Sarah, saw she was awake, eyes regarding him seriously.

'I've been dreaming we're lost in the bayou,' she said. 'Seems it's true.' She studied her grubby hands. Ran fingers through her matted hair. 'Next time you decide to ask for a favour, Jason Brand, please don't.'

'What do you want me to say?'

She scowled briefly. Shook her head. 'How about telling me to quit grumbling?'

He leaned over and kissed her quickly. 'We'd better move out.'

The sound reached them at that precise moment. Someone moving through the heavy undergrowth. Sarah glanced at Brand, a question beginning to form on her lips. He waved her to silence. Pulling the revolver from his belt Brand moved towards the sound.

The man was alone. He carried a rifle. Though he moved with the confidence of a man at ease with his surroundings there was nervousness in his face. He plainly didn't like the idea of creeping around the bayou on the trail of a known hostile fugitive. His unease made him vulnerable and Brand used that to his advantage. He closed on the man, reaching him unseen and pressed the Colt's muzzle against the side of the man's head.

'Breath easy, friend, it'll keep you alive longer,' Brand advised, reaching to take the man's rifle. Over his shoulder he called to Sarah.

She came to his side. Brand passed her the rifle, then searched the man for additional weapons. Found a holstered revolver and a sheathed knife.

'Take off the coat,' Brand told his captive. He took the offered garment and handed it to Sarah. She slipped it on gratefully. 'Turn round, friend,' Brand said.

The man did as he was told. His expression was sullen, but any anger he carried he kept suppressed, because he knew how much this man had done already and he had no desire to become the next casualty.

'Easy question,' Brand said. 'How many others are there looking for us?'

The man shrugged. 'Seven. Eight. Maybe more. Ain't certain.'

'Dogs still out?'

The man shook his head. 'They took 'em back a while ago. Couldn't pick up a scent.'

'One more question, friend, and I figure you already know what it is. Just make sure you answer right.'

Despite his reservations not to make things difficult for himself the man shook his head stubbornly.

'No way I'm telling you where the cache is.'

Brand didn't even think about what he did. He simply slammed the barrel of the revolver down across the bridge of the man's nose. Bone cracked and blood spurted down the front of the man's shirt. He gasped in pain, pulling back, but not fast enough to avoid Brand's fist. It clubbed him across the jaw and drove him to his knees. He knelt in the wet mud, groaning.

'I can keep this up as long as you want,' Brand said.

The man stared up at him, blinking tears of pain from his eyes. 'I'm a dead man if St Clair finds out I talked.'

'Friend, you can still be a dead man if you *don't* talk.'

The man considered his options. If he did take this man to the cache he might still get out alive. There were guards at the hiding place. Maybe they could stop this crazy Northerner.

'I'll take you there,' he said.

Brand hauled the man to his feet. He shoved both revolvers under his belt. Tucked the knife in the top of his boot and retrieved the rifle from Sarah.

'Let's move out.'

The man moved ahead of them, deeper into the bayou. He cast about for a while before he found his way, then settled into a steady walk, confident of his bearings. Brand saw no difference in their surroundings, except that they were walking on solid ground all the time. Their man obviously knew his way around the swamp.

They walked for a long time. The sun rose high overhead. Heat filtered down through the greenery. The steamy heat clung to them. Insects appeared in swarms, searching them out in droves. Out of sight things splashed in the dank waters.

They had been travelling for at least two hours when the man came to a dead stop.

'There a problem?' Brand asked, moving up behind the man, leaning the muzzle of the rifle against the man's spine.

The man pointed. 'The cache is just ahead. Big cave in back of a waterfall on the far side of a pool. You can hear the water.'

Brand noticed the sound now.

'Any guards?'

'*No!*' The man's answer came too quickly and Brand knew he was lying. St Clair wouldn't have left a valuable cache of arms unprotected. The captive wanted Brand to walk in unaware.

'Hey,' Brand said softly.

When the man turned Brand whacked him across the head with the rifle, dropping him like a stone. Turning him on his face Brand stripped off the man's belt and tied his hands. He tore a strip of cloth from the unconscious man's shirt and used it to gag him.

'Maybe you should wait here,' Brand suggested to Sarah.

The look in her eyes told him it was not a wise suggestion.

'Come on then,' he said grudgingly. 'Let's see if we can start the day with a bang.'

8

Crouching knee deep in brackish water Brand studied the movements of the two men guarding the entrance to the cave. It was fronted by a pool of sorts. A wide stretch of scummy water that seemed to be alive with swamp life. On the far side a rocky bluff, covered with greenery, rose high into the mass of trees, with a thin fall of water spilling over its rim. The water dropped straight down, shielding the mouth of the dark cave.

'Jason,' Sarah whispered.

'What?'

'I don't want to make a fuss, but there appears to be a snake swimming this way.'

Brand took her arm and moved her aside. Thick mud lay beneath their feet, under the foul smelling water. Each time they took a step the disturbed slime released trapped gas. It rose to the surface, bubbling and releasing sulphurous fumes. They reached solid ground again and edged through the tangled undergrowth. Brand settled Sarah then returned to study the cave area again.

To one side of the cave was a crude hut. It appeared that St Clair had a permanent presence watching over the weapons cache.

He checked out his handguns, making sure they were both loaded. He handed the rifle back to Sarah.

'Can you handle one of these?'

'I can usually hit what I aim at,' she said sharply. 'But I've never had to shoot at a man before.'

'I'm hoping you don't have to. I just want you to stay here. Keep your ears and eyes open. If you do see anything that doesn't look right use the damn rifle. Don't think about it. Just shoot. You either want to stay alive or you don't.'

She scowled at him. 'Do my best to

uphold the honour of the damn regiment, *sir!*'

Brand leaned across and kissed her. 'Lady Sarah, you'd make a mean man.'

'Wouldn't be as much fun in bed though.'

'You could be right.'

'Jason — be careful.'

He eased through the undergrowth, skirting the edge of the pool, his eyes always monitoring the movements of the two guards. He was grateful for the thick tangle of greenery that grew across the whole area. It covered his movements. He could hear the guards' voices carrying over the pool. They didn't seem to be all that content. Being stuck out here in the bayou had unsettled them. Brand hoped it had made them lax.

One of the guards sat on a rotted stump and started to roll himself a smoke. The other man said something to him, tucked his rifle under his arm and wandered across to the shack. He went inside. Shortly smoke began to rise from the crude chimney stack angled crookedly from the sloping roof of the shack.

Brand kept moving until he was within a few yards of the rear of the shack. He could hear the man inside the shack moving around, mumbling to himself. The tantalising aroma of frying bacon reached Brand's nostrils making him realise how hungry he was.

He pushed thoughts of food to the back of his mind as he concentrated on the guard sitting on the tree stump, smoking his cigarette. The man's rifle lay across his knees, so he wasn't in any position for a quick response. That suited Brand. He wasn't about to give the guard any kind of chance — but anything could go wrong.

Once he had made up his mind Brand moved. He took long strides, bringing him up behind the guard, and slammed the barrel of his revolver down across the man's skull. As the guard began to slump Brand hit him again, snatching up the falling rifle as it slid toward the ground. He also took the guard's handgun, tossing both weapons into the pool.

Turning in toward the shack Brand was unexpectedly confronted by the second guard as he stepped out of the door. The guard locked eyes with the intruder and went for his holstered gun. Brand raised the Colt in his fist, dogging back the hammer and tripping the trigger.

The gun misfired.

Still moving forward, even as the gun became a dead weight in his hand, Brand didn't waste time on a second attempt. He lunged at the guard, ducking low. He heard the man's gun fire, the heat of the shot scorching his cheek as he slammed shoulder first into the guard's stomach. The momentum propelled them back through the shack's open door. As they stumbled inside they struck something that splintered beneath their weight, sending them crashing to the floor. Breaking free Brand pushed to his feet, and saw the outline of the other's gun lifting again. He kicked out, the toe of his boot catching the man's gunhand. A yell of pain split the air as the weapon spun from his fingers. He swore angrily, recovering fast and came up off the floor with a slim bladed knife in his free hand. He held it low, body crouching as he watched Brand. When he moved he was fast, the slender blade slicing through Brand's sleeve, scoring the flesh. Blood soaked Brand's shirt. The guard moved in again, weaving, the blade glittering as it cut the air, then thrust forward. This time the cut was to Brand's chest. The guard knew how to use a knife, and his skill was making him confident. Sure that he had Brand where he wanted him.

Brand felt heat at his back. Remembered the plume of smoke he had seen rising from the chimney. He recalled the smell of frying bacon. There was a cook stove behind him. He let his eyes flick to the left and saw the small, round-bodied cast iron stove close by.

His glance took in the heavy iron fry pan sitting atop the stove. Thick slices of salted bacon crackled in the hot fat of the fry pan.

He acted without any further thought, spinning on his heel and snatching up the heavy pan and swinging back toward the startled guard. Brand hurled the contents of the pan into the guard's face.

The man's scream was loud, shrill. He stumbled away from Brand, dropping the knife as he clasped both hands to his burned, blistering face. The scalding fat had burned deep into his flesh, searing skin and eyes.

Brand snatched up the man's fallen gun. He eased back the hammer, raised the weapon and put a single shot through the back of the screaming man's skull, ending his agony.

Stepping outside Brand made for the cave. Fine spray soaked his shirt as he made his way across the wet stone ledge behind the waterfall. The cave before him was a dark hole pushing deep into the rock. Oil lamps hung on metal spikes driven into the rock. Brand took one and returned to the guard he'd knocked unconscious. He found matches in the man's pocket and used one to light his lamp.

It didn't take him long to find what he was looking for.

Only yards inside the cave were stacked boxes and crates. Even barrels. A quick check confirmed Brand's suspicions. They contained large quantities of weapons. Rifles and handguns. There was ammunition. Black powder. Even bullet moulds and lead strip. It was an impressive and frightening arsenal. It showed that Beauregard St Clair did things on a grand scale.

Brand spotted something familiar off to the side. It was one of the Gatling Guns he had seen in St Clair's cellar. The gun had been fully assembled and loaded. Beside the weapon was an open box containing additional magazines. The Gatling was pointing at the cave entrance. Most probably there as a safeguard to protect the arms cache if it was discovered.

Hanging the lamp on a wall spike Brand returned to the stored weapons. He took a couple of black powder casks and used the butt of his handgun to break the tops. He laid a thick trail of powder around the other powder casks and the ammunition boxes. Then he used the remaining powder in the second cask to lay a thick line of powder across the floor of the cave, taking it to the mouth of the cave.

He realised it was a waste of good munitions, but better to destroy it all than let any of it stay in St Clair's hands. There was no way Brand could let McCord know what he'd found. And St Clair's people weren't far behind. If the man spirited the weapons away they might vanish completely. The man was fanatic enough to have his supporters use the weapons, so Brand decided to remove temptation. Someone in Washington would raise all hell over the waste of Government property. Brand wasn't going to waste too much time letting that worry him.

He stood at the mouth of the cave, studying the powder trail, wondering how long it would take for it to burn. When it did reach the arms cache there was going to be an impressive explosion, and Brand wanted to be at a fair distance when that happened.

He took the oil lamp, preparing to touch off the powder.

And froze.

Was that his imagination? Or had he heard someone call his name? He turned in the direction of the cave's mouth, and heard the shout clearly this time.

'We know you're in there, Brand! Show yourself! And do it fast because we have your lady friend with us! Alive — for now!'

9

Sarah hadn't even heard them!

The first indication that she had been discovered had been a rough hand grasping her arm and yanking her to her feet. Someone spun her round. The rifle had been torn from her grasp. She got a quick impression of a group of men, at least eight of them. And among them was the pale, slim figure of Willard St Clair.

Sarah's first thought was of Brand. She opened her mouth to yell a warning, but a heavy fist struck her. She stumbled back from the blow, tasting blood in her mouth and the sting of a cut lip.

'If I was you, Miss Debenham, I would maintain a dignified silence.'

Sarah glared at Willard St Clair. A shudder ran through her. There was something repellent about him. The unhealthy way he was staring at her made her uneasy.

'I say we should get over to the shack,' one of the men said.

Sarah saw it was the man Brand had forced to lead them to this place.

Willard silenced him with a flick of his hand. 'In time, Bates. In time.' He moved closer to Sarah. 'First I need to find out something from our guest.'

'Go to hell!' Sarah told him.

'Damned if she ain't got guts,' one of the other men said.

The observation failed to impress Willard.

'If I were you, my dear lady, I would temper my words with caution.'

'Fine,' Sarah replied. 'Would you kindly go to hell.'

A man laughed. Willard's face paled even more. He took a short breath, then lashed out with his slender hand. The blow stung Sarah's cheek. Tears of pain filled her eyes. She forced herself to face Willard.

'If I was a man you wouldn't have

dared to do that. The only reason you managed to hit me now was because all these men are behind you.'

'You damn Yankee bitch!' Willard screamed, his voice rising to a girlish squeal. 'At least you're right about one thing. If you *were* a man I wouldn't be able to do this . . . '

He reached out to snatch at her shirt, ripping it from shoulder to waist and exposing her naked body. Before Sarah could move away from him Willard cupped one of her breasts, his thin fingers squeezing cruelly. Sarah gasped as his nails dug into her soft flesh.

'Now you tell me, girl. Who is that man? I know he's not Colter. Believe me it would be better if you told me what I need to know. Every man here has been out searching all night, and they're all aching for a chance to spend some time with you.'

Bates pushed forward, eyes gleaming. He dragged the coat off Sarah's shoulders.

'I'll have this back first.' Then he

grinned. 'And I might take the pants to go with them.'

He began to paw at Sarah's belt, his hands sliding over her stomach and thighs.

'Your choice,' Willard said. 'No help coming so you can yell all you want. Tell the truth, girl, I'll enjoy watching the boys havin' their fun.'

Sarah held out for a few minutes, until the sweaty touch of so many hands was too much for her to bear. She felt guilty. Weak at her capitulation, but the implicit threats coming from the grinning bunch of men made her aware of what they had in store for her, and it was too much.

'So he's a damned government agent!'

Willard rounded on the man who had spoken.

'What does it matter who he is? He's helpless out here. No way he can get a message to his people. He isn't going to get out alive so anything he's learned dies here in the bayou along with him.'

'If he's an agent it means the government must know what we're planning.'

'If they come we'll kill them too,' Willard raged. 'And I don't believe they know too much. If they did they wouldn't have sent one man. I believe we're safe as long as we kill this man Brand. He's been sent to try and find out what we're doing. All he's got are some stolen guns. Nothing else.'

'We could lose them if he takes a mind to destroy them,' Bates pointed out. 'Took us a long time to collect them. Your daddy ain't goin' to be too happy if Brand blows those guns sky high.'

Willard calmed down, staring at Bates, because even he could see the logic of the man's argument.

'All right. Let's move. And fetch the woman along. She might be able to persuade him to come out peacefully.'

'Unless Quinn and Prentice have already stopped him,' one man suggested.

Bates dragged Sarah to her feet. 'Not that bastard. He's mean enough to have taken Quinn and Prentice without breakin' sweat.'

When they reached the pool, gazing across the tranquil water, they were able to see the motionless figure stretched out near the shack.

'Told you so,' Bates said, rounding on Willard. 'Where is he, St Clair? My money says inside the damn cave.'

'Shut your mouth,' Willard yelled. 'Let me figure this out. Then *I'll* tell you what to do.'

Bates held back with difficulty. He didn't like Willard. The man was a weak fool. He liked to throw his weight about, using his father's authority as a shield. His problem was he caved in too easily when the pressure was on him.

'*Well, what do we do now, boss-man?*' Bates taunted after a short wait.

'Bring the girl,' Willard ordered.

Sarah was hauled to the pool's edge and a challenge yelled in the direction of the cave. Clutching her torn clothing against her bruised, trembling body, Sarah hoped Brand *was* inside. She wished she could have been with him. Anything would have been preferable to the bunch of braying men jostling around her.

'Maybe he ain't there,' one man said.

'Sweet Jesus,' Bates said. 'Of course the bastard's in there. You expect him to show and wave at us, Anderson?'

'Bates,' Willard said. 'Put your knife to the girl's throat.'

Bates grinned. This was something he liked. He took a knife from one of the men and grabbed Sarah by the hair, forcing her to her knees. Moving behind her he pulled her head back and laid the keen edge of the blade against her taut throat.

'I know you're in there, Brand,' Willard called out. 'If you don't want to see the woman's throat sliced open show yourself. And be quick about it.'

Despite the knife at her throat Sarah struggled against Bates' restraining grip. He pushed against even harder.

'You go right on squirming, honey,' Bates whispered, crouching low behind her. He was enjoying the pressure of her firm buttocks against his groin. 'Right now this is the best part of the day.'

There was no response from the cave. Silence apart from the hiss of the falling water.

'Brand?'

Nothing.

Willard St Clair began to sweat. *Why wasn't Brand responding?* Maybe the woman didn't mean that much to him after all. It was possible the man would allow her to die.

Before any further thoughts passed through Willard's confused mind there *was* a response from within the cave. It was far from anything he might have expected, but it confirmed one thing.

Jason Brand was still around, and he was in no mood to talk.

He let something else do his talking for him, and it tore the day wide open with deadly intent.

10

Brand had dragged the assembled Gatling Gun to the mouth of the cave along with the box of extra magazines.

When Willard and his men appeared Brand stood back and waited to see what they were going to do.

He watched as one of the men pushed Sarah to her knees and laid a knife to her throat.

The main bunch were standing to one side, giving him a clear line of fire. Brand knew what he had to do. Willard was giving him no choice.

They knew who he was. By now they would have figured out the reason for his presence. Which meant the moment he stepped out of the cave he was a dead man.

Sarah was also under threat. Brand knew they would kill her too. And no amount of bleating from McCord would change anything once they were dead. So Brand had to make his choices here and now, and act on them.

He had opened one of the cases and selected a brand new Colt Peacemaker. Wiping off the thin coat of oil with the tail of his shirt Brand had broken open a carton of .45 calibre shells and loaded the gun. He had tucked the weapon under his belt, dropping a handful of cartridges in his pants pocket. The burning lamp, with the glass raised, stood beside him as he tugged the Gatling round to line up on the main group of men just beyond Sarah and Willard St Clair. He checked that the weapon was primed and ready, then reached for the cranking handle.

So you want to start a war do you? Want the Confederacy to rise again? So try this for size!

He cranked the handle.

The Gatling exploded with sound. The cylinder of barrels rotated, each one spitting out a bullet as it passed the breech. The cave reverberated to the chatter of gunfire. Smoke filled the air. Through the haze of the waterfall Brand saw a line of bullets march across the pool, bursts of foam lifting. He tilted the barrel as he kept firing and this time saw his stream of fire rip into the bunched men even as they tried to scatter. He angled the barrel left and right, catching them as they spread. They went down in a yelling mass, bodies punctured and bloody.

Willard suddenly broke out of his motionless trance. Turning to Sarah he snatched at her arm, dragging her to her feet and used her as a shield as he retreated into the undergrowth, followed by the man who had been holding the knife to Sarah's throat.

Brand let go of the cranking handle. He picked up the oil lamp and turned up the wick. He touched the flame to the trail of black powder. It crackled and spat, then gushed out a long tail of bright flame. With surprising speed it began to race toward the main stack of weapons and the additional powder

Brand had spread around.

Aware that time was running out fast Brand turned and made for the mouth of the cave, through the waterfall and skirted the edge of the pool. He was making for the rear of the shack. The only cover close by.

The blast came before he reached the shack.

The sound of the explosion was deafening.

The ground shook beneath Brand's feet. A gush of flame and smoke belched from the mouth of the cave. The air was suddenly full of flying debris. The impact of the blast picked Brand up and threw him for yards. He landed face down, rolling frantically to break his fall. The day turned dark as the boiling smoke from the explosion spilled over him, followed by the heat of the blast.

Brand lay for long moments. He was shaking from head to foot. Moments later he felt a mist of cool water drizzle over him. Probably the contents of the pool. He raised his aching head.

A pall of thick smoke drifted over the area. The shack had been torn apart. It lay a splintered wreck, flames licking at the wooden frame. The mouth of the cave was piled high with shattered rock.

Brand climbed to his feet, feeling giddy until his senses sorted themselves out. He pulled the Colt from his belt. Cocked it.

He made his way round to the far side of the pool. Willard's men lay in bloody rags. Not a man was moving. Brand stepped by them, making his way to where Willard had vanished in the undergrowth. Before long he found a bunch of tethered horses. He chose one and swung into the saddle. He cast around until he found the fresh tracks left by Willard and his man. One of the horses was carrying double.

They still had Sarah with them!

Willard was moving fast. Making no attempt to cover his trail. Which made it easier for Brand to follow. Willard plainly knew the bayou well.

Brand knew where he would be heading. Back home. To tell his father what had happened. Willard would have heard the explosion. It wouldn't take much intelligence to guess what had happened. Beauregard St Clair was not going to take the news of his arms cache being destroyed very well. He was going to have to do some drastic rethinking. To alter his plans — whatever they were. He would also have to convince his backers that the St Clair plan was still in operation, despite the loss of valuable weapons.

So what would St Clair do next? He would have some kind of contingency plan set up. St Clair was that kind of man. Something to show he was still the man to lead the Brotherhood.

Brand spurred his horse on. The sooner he reached the St Clair mansion the sooner he might find out what St Clair had planned next.

And more importantly he would be where Sarah was.

11

He left the horse some distance from the house, moving in on foot. As he neared the place he became aware of the silence. The St Clair mansion gave the appearance of being deserted. Then Brand spotted two horses, heads hanging from exhaustion, standing near the front entrance.

He checked the Colt, making sure it was ready for use, then covered the final distance to the house at a run. Movement off to his right caught his eye. He turned, the revolver rising in his hand, but all he saw was a lace curtain blowing through an open window.

The large front doors stood wide open. They seemed to be beckoning him to enter.

Brand reached the doors and stepped through quickly, moving to one side the moment he was inside.

In that instant a gun blasted at him from the landing on the first floor. Someone in the shadows at the top of the stairs. The bullet exploded plaster from the wall inches from his head. Splinters stung his flesh. Brand dropped to one knee and returned fire. His bullet whined off something hard. He picked up the sound of retreating footsteps. Brand broke away from the wall and went up the stairs two at a time. Reaching the landing he turned and cut off along the adjoining passage. He spotted a dark figure at the far end of the passage. The figure paused, turning, a dull gleam of light bouncing off the barrel of a raised gun. They fired together. Brand felt the burn of a bullet across the back of his hand. Blood began to flow almost immediately. With a reflex action Brand fired a second time, snapping off his shot almost without aiming, and saw the distant figure jerk to one side. Bounce off the wall. Despite the severe wound the man braced himself to return fire, hauling his heavy gun up with both hands. Extending his gunarm Brand fired twice more, hard hammered shots that caught the target in the side of the head. The man went down hard, his gun bouncing from his fingers as he struck the floor. He twisted over on his back, moaning in pain. Blood began to pool under his head. He shuddered for a short time, then became still.

Flipping open the loading gate Brand ejected the spent cartridges and thumbed in fresh loads. He stayed put, ears and eyes straining to pick up anything that might tell him where Willard and Sarah were. They were close, he knew that.

The silence stretched out. The house was too quiet. Brand could hear his own breathing. The soft rustle of his clothing each time he moved.

His wait was short.

From one of the rooms along the passage came a sudden crash. A heavy piece of furniture being overturned. A man cried out, and Brand recognised the shrill sound.

Willard St Clair.

There was no mistake. Brand headed along the passage, seeking the source of the sound.

A door burst open and a familiar figure ran into the passage. It was Sarah. She saw him, eyes wide with a mix of pleasure and fright. Her mouth began to form a warning.

From inside the room a gun fired, the heavy crash of sound filling the passage. Sarah cried out in terror as the bullet struck her between the shoulders. The force pushed her forward, knocking her off balance, and Brand watched in horror as Sarah tumbled to the floor, arms outstretched. Her face had become twisted in shock. The bullet burst out of her body in a shower of bloody debris, ripping through her left breast. Blood and shredded cloth spattered the wall. She struck the floor and rolled up against the base of the wall.

As his shock evaporated Brand was overcome by a surge of bestial violence.

The slim figure of Willard St Clair had appeared in the door of the room. He still clutched the smoking gun in his pale hand. He was part way through the door when Brand triggered the Colt, driving a bullet in Willard's left shoulder. The powerful lead slug shattered bone, spinning Willard around in a half-circle. His face slammed into the doorframe as he twisted around. He bounced off the frame, stumbling to the floor, dazed and in pain, blood dribbling from his mouth. He slumped on his knees, the gun in his hand forgotten. Brand allowed him no time to remember. He reached Willard's hunched figure, swinging the Colt in a smashing arc that struck the man's gunhand, cracking bone and numbing his grip. Willard looked up into Brand's taut, angry face, a whimper of terror bubbling from his throat as he recognised the look in Brand's eyes. He tried to shrink away from the swinging gun, but it chopped up and down, each blow opening a fresh, bleeding gash. Scuttling backwards, like a retreating crab, Willard slithered across the floor. At one point he gained his feet, half rising before Brand's blows sent him sprawling again. As Willard crashed to the floor again Brand cast aside the blood slick Colt and bent over the man. He hauled Willard to his feet and used his fists, beating the whimpering figure to a bloody, broken wreck. Only when his anger subsided did he stop, allowing Willard to curl up in a shuddering heap on the floor.

Brand stood over the moaning figure, fists at his sides, his chest heaving from his exertions. He felt lost. Out of place in this great empty house.

And then suddenly reality forced itself back into his conscious mind and he turned to where Sarah still lay. He turned her over gently, scared that he would find she was dead. But the faint movement of her chest told him otherwise. The front of her shirt was sodden with blood and he could hardly bear to look at the terrible wound. A thin trickle of blood stained the corner of her mouth. Without warning her eyes opened and she stared up at him.

'He was waiting to shoot you,' she said softly, as if it explained everything. 'I had to do something.' Her voice was so low he had to bend over her to hear.

'Don't try to talk,' he said. He was thinking how pale she looked. And there was so much damned blood.

He heard a soft footstep close by. Turning, his anger growing again Brand checked himself as he recognised Frederick, the Negro who had welcomed them to the St Clair mansion on their arrival.

'Frederick, the lady needs a doctor. Fast.'

The Negro knelt beside Sarah. His dark, lined face was grave as he looked across at Brand.

'Nearest one is at Blanchville. Doctor Tealer.'

'How far?'

'Take about an hour to get there, sir.'

Brand pushed to his feet. 'There a carriage around here?'

'Yes, sir,' Frederick said. He inclined his head in Willard's direction.

'Only be room for one in the carriage.'

'He isn't going to be needing a doctor,' Brand said coldly.

Frederick nodded in understanding. He stood up.

'I'll get the carriage.' He turned away then glanced back at Brand. 'The Senator and Mister Royce left a few hours ago. Far as I could tell they were making for New Orleans. That any help, sir?'

'Could be, Frederick. Thanks.'

'You're welcome, sir. If you can make the lady comfortable I'll bring the carriage and drive her to Blanchville myself.'

'You sure?'

'The way I see it, sir, you have things to do, and you don't have all that much time to do them.'

'You could be right.' As Frederick moved away Brand asked: 'What about Lucilla? She still here?'

'No, sir. She's gone as well. Same time as her father.'

While Frederick arranged the carriage Brand did what he could for Sarah. Feeling less than competent he tried to slow the bleeding and managed after a fashion. As he was doing this Sarah slipped into unconsciousness. Her condition worried him. More so because he was unable to do anything about it. When Frederick returned he had a young Negro girl with him. They had brought along blankets. Brand and Frederick carried Sarah downstairs and outside. A thick mattress of pillows had been arranged in the carriage. They placed Sarah inside, covered her with blankets, the girl climbing in beside her. Frederick took the seat and picked up the reins.

'With the help of the Lord we'll get her there, sir,' the Negro said.

Brand watched the carriage roll away down the long drive. He had a greater faith in Frederick than the Negro had in the Lord.

Back in the house Brand climbed the stairs and made his way back to where he had left Willard. He scooped up his Colt and turned to where the young St Clair had dragged himself to his feet to stand slumped against the wall. He stared at Brand through a mask of blood and held his battered hands crossed over his stained shirt.

'Just one question, you son of a bitch. Where's your father gone? And don't waste my time by lying.'

Willard didn't say a word. Brand hit him full in the mouth. Blood flew in a froth from Willard's swollen lips.

'I can keep this up longer than you can take it,' Brand said.

Willard took a wild swing at him. Brand weaved to one side, then punched Willard again, knocking him to his knees. Willard swayed drunkenly, trying to stand up. He fell back against the wall.

'If that stupid bitch hadn't got in my way I would have killed you! I hope she dies and goes to hell . . . '

Brand snapped up the Colt and fired a single shot. The bullet shattered Willard's left kneecap. Bloody chunks of flesh hung from the ruined limb. Willard screamed and clutched his hands over the seething wound, blood seeping through his fingers.

'No! I won't tell you a damn thing.' he yelled defiantly.

Brand cocked the Colt again. 'This is taking Southern honour too far, boy,' he said.

'Yankee trash!'

The Colt kicked back as Brand fired again. Willard's right leg jerked under the impact of the .45 calibre slug. Willard curled up in a ball, hugging himself to make the pain go away.

The sound of the Colt's hammer going back once more sounded loud in the silence.

'For God's sake, Brand,' Willard pleaded.

'Where's your father?'

Willard pushed himself into a semi-sitting position, leaving a trail of slick blood on the floor as he moved. He gazed up at Brand through eyes wide with pain.

'Washington. Royce and my father have gone to Washington.'

'Something for the Brotherhood?'

Willard's face hardened.

'They have something to do. You won't stop them.' Willard's battered face creased into a terrible smile. 'They'll show you all the Brotherhood is real.'

'By doing what?'

Willard began to laugh. High and hysterical, the sound bounced off the panelled walls. It made Brand shiver.

'You'll see on the fourteenth,' Willard said. 'April fourteenth. You won't forget that day.'

He was still laughing. An insane sound that rose until it blotted out everything else.

And then the laughing stopped. Willard stared directly at Brand. He knew he had said too much. Even through his pain the realisation sobered him.

'Damn you,' he said bitterly. A surge of pain racked his slender body and he clutched himself. 'For pity's sake, Brand, help me. I'm in bad pain. Give me something to stop it, man.'

The smile on Jason Brand's face was *almost* human.

'I aim to, boy. I really do,' he said, and put two bullets through Willard's skull.

12

He made his way through the silent house to the room he'd been using. Changing into clean clothes Brand strapped on the shoulder harness and checked that the Colt Special was loaded before he put it away. He buckled on his waist belt but found that the Colt he'd taken from the cache had too long a barrel for the holster. Making his way back downstairs he sought out St Clair's study. Maybe he could find an extra handgun there.

He kicked open the heavy door. It slammed back against the inner wall with a solid thump. The quietness unsettled him. Had everyone on the estate run off?

Crossing the study he paused before the liquor cabinet, helping himself to a bottle of expensive bourbon. His long swallow burned its way to the pit of his stomach. He gasped, his eyes brimming with tears. The liquor made him cough. He'd been a fool to drink on an empty stomach. He threw the bottle across the room in an angry gesture. It smashed against the wall, glass exploding in an amber spray.

Brand slumped behind St Clair's big desk, methodically dragging open the drawers and dumping the contents out before him. He aimlessly sorted through the stuff, not even knowing what he was looking for. Papers fell to the floor. In his anger Brand became clumsier. He was wasting time. Achieving nothing, and his anger was because he could not erase the image of Sarah from his mind. Sarah hurt and in pain because he had dragged her into his world of violence and brutal treachery. His fault. All of it. He swept the top of the desk clear with a violent motion, sending everything across the floor. He sat for a moment, his eyes searching the room until he saw the glass fronted gun cabinet standing against one wall.

He stood before the cabinet, staring at the racked guns, the pistols suspended from brass hooks. He didn't open the doors. Simply smashed the thin glass with his clenched fist, reaching inside to take a cedar-handled Colt .45 off its hook. It was the same model as the one he'd lost. It was not brand new but it had been well cared for. The balance was perfect, the oiled action smooth and sure. He loaded the weapon and dropped it into his holster, then turned and strode out of the study and the house.

He went to the stables. Picking out a horse he saddled up and rode away from the St Clair estate, locating the New Orleans road. He had a good ride ahead of him and even when he reached the place he had a long train journey to endure.

Brand reviewed the information he had. St Clair and Royce had taken off for New Orleans. But that didn't mean they would stay there. Brand had wrecked the arms cache, leaving the

Brotherhood short on weapons. Unless they had other caches. Willard's words rattled around in Brand's head. His statement about the Brotherhood still being able to show their strength. Still being a force to be reckoned with. What had he meant?

April the fourteenth?

What was the significance of the date? Brand felt he should know.

He reached New Orleans late. He located a livery stable and left the horse there. Then he searched out a telegraph office and sent a telegram to McCord, bringing him up to date. He also mentioned St Clair's visit to Washington, hoping McCord might be able to figure out what the date meant.

Making his way to the rail depot he bought a through ticket to Washington, then found he had three hours to wait. He also realised he was hungry. With no particular destination in mind he wandered around until he found a decent restaurant. He ordered a steak with all the trimmings and a pot of coffee. Despite lingering over the meal he found he still had almost two hours before train time.

Brand retraced his steps to the depot. Nearing the depot he found himself walking along a narrow, littered street that bordered the freight yards. There was little light in this part of town. The air had a smoky, sooty tang to it, and in the distance he heard the mournful wail of a departing train. His boots crunched on the gravel that lay underfoot, the sound echoing behind him.

Echoing!

Echoing like hell! Not in an open space like this!

Brand stopped, turning on his heels, hearing them coming on fast now he had sensed their closeness.

He counted three of them. Dark shapes moving fast, and he knew they were out to stop him, one way or another. Brand's right slid under his coat, bringing out the shoulder-holstered Colt. He barely had time to ease back the hammer before the lead man slammed into him. The assailant was big, solid, and the impact spun Brand backwards. He stumbled, losing his balance and dropped to his knees. There was a moment when he almost lost his grip on the Colt, but he caught his balance, steadied himself. The big man had pulled out a thick-bladed knife, cold steel gleaming in the pale light. Brand didn't hesitate. He lifted the Colt and drove three fast shots into the man's wide body. The target was lifted off his feet by the force of the heavy .45 calibre bullets. He arched over with a gurgle of sound, dark gouts of blood spurting from the wounds as he crashed to the hard ground.

Movement off to Brand's left registered in the corner of his eye. He twisted round. Too slow. Something smashed across the back of his neck, driving him face down in the dirt, flesh scraped from his cheek. A boot slammed into his side, flipping him over on his back. Brand gasped in pain, heard a man laugh in triumph. The Colt was booted from his hand. He didn't try for his waist gun yet. No time. He was too busy rolling away from the flailing boots intent on kicking him to death. He had realised that these men were were little more than street brawlers. Not professional assassins. A bullet in the back of the head would have been Brand's first indication of professionals. Somebody had paid this trio to deal with him, but they hadn't picked too well. Not that it made the pain any easier to bear. It only meant he had an edge over them.

The moment he got a couple of clear seconds Brand gathered himself and pushed up off the ground. He was ready as the remaining pair closed in again, still grinning like the idiots they were. As they narrowed the gap Brand struck. The toe of his boot caught one directly between his legs, the force of the kick lifting the man off his feet. He staggered back, bellowing like a stricken bull, then dropped to his knees, clutching at his groin. The noise distracted the third one. As he paused, glancing at his hurt partner Brand sledged the edge of his left hand across the man's throat. The crippling impact crushed every bone in the man's throat and made it almost impossible to breath. He lost interest in the whole affair, clawing at his throat, eyes bulging. The last thing the man saw was the barrel of Brand's Colt as it slid clear of the holster. The muzzle flickered with flame, the bullet slamming into the man's skull. He toppled over backwards, dead before he hit the ground.

Brand turned to the moaning survivor. The man was still on his knees, head hanging. Brand caught a handful of the man's long, greasy hair and yanked his head up. The face was twisted in agony, tears streaming from the man's eyes. He was dribbling like a hurt child. He gave a startled cry when Brand jammed the muzzle of the Colt hard against his cheek.

'You feel that?'

The man stared at him as if Brand wasn't even speaking English. Brand slapped the side of his face with the Colt, just hard enough to hurt.

'Feel it now?' he asked.

The man nodded. 'I hurt,' he moaned, clutching at his groin.

'That's because I kicked you in the balls, friend, and if I don't get the answer I want I'm liable to shoot 'em off. One by one. Understand?'

'*Jesus Christ!*' the man mumbled.

'He can't help you,' Brand said. 'Only me.'

It only took a look into Brand's cold, empty eyes to convince the man.

'Who hired you?'

The man sighed. It wasn't that hard a question. The job was over, so there was no point in getting hurt any more.

'A young woman. She gave us your description and a big wad of money. Told us to wait around the depot. If you showed we was to wait our chance and do for you.'

'What did she look like?'

'Fair hair. A real looker. Smelled of money.'

Lucilla St Clair.

It appeared that the young woman was still looking out for her father's interests.

'Anyone with her?'

The man shrugged. 'If there was we didn't see.' He hesitated. 'Hey, mister, what are you going to do?'

Brand released him and straightened up. 'I'm going to catch my train,' he said.

Anger shadowed the man's face. 'The hell with your damn train. What about me?'

'You had your shot,' Brand said coldly. 'You missed.'

The Colt's barrel moved slightly, the hammer going back with a soft sound. The man on the ground twisted his head around, eyes wide with shock as he realised what was about to happen. That was as far as he got. The .45 crackled with sound and the man was flung over on his back with a bullet through his heart.

Retrieving his Colt Special Brand walked away from the scene and continued on his way back to the depot. He dusted himself off as he approached the empty waiting room and settled down on a hard bench, facing the door, his aching back pressed against the wall. His train arrived five minutes behind schedule. Brand climbed on board and a Negro attendant showed him to the private apartment he'd booked. Brand locked his door, stripped off his coat and shirt and washed. The water was cold, but it took away the cobwebs that were threatening to dull his senses. As he dried himself he took a look in the mirror. There were fresh bruises down the side of his body, almost to the waist, and his face had looked better. He grinned at his reflection in the mirror. No damn wonder the attendant had kept giving him sidelong glances.

Sitting on the edge of the apartment's fixed bunk he reloaded both of his revolvers, then pulled his shirt back on and stretched out on the bunk, staring out of the window as the train eased away from New Orleans. There was a long ride ahead, with a change of locomotive at Atlanta. He felt the train picking up speed and saw the city lights fall behind, dimming in the enveloping darkness. Slipping the Colt special under his pillow Brand lay down and pulled the blankets over him. He needed sleep but it refused to come. His mind kept conjuring up images of Sarah. Inactivity allowed his mind to fix on her. He felt guilty for having involved her in the affair. It hadn't been his intention. Her part was simply to gain him an introduction to St Clair. With his past record maybe he should have left her out. Life had a nasty habit of jumping the rails and going off along other tracks, mostly out of control. And when that did happen people got hurt — usually those who shouldn't have been there in the first instance. He stirred restlessly, attempting to push the

152

thoughts out of his mind and finally drifted into an exhausted sleep.

He woke to a knocking on the apartment door. When he opened it he came face to face with the Negro attendant.

'Morning, sir. You want some breakfast?'

Brand nodded. He scrubbed a hand across his stubbled face.

'Any chance of a razor?'

'Leave it to me, sir.' The attendant turned to go. 'We make a stop in about ten minutes. Small town. Anything you need, sir?'

Brand remembered his torn, soiled shirt. He picked up his coat and took out his wallet. Pulling out a number of bills he handed them to the waiting attendant.

'Clean shirt. I'll leave it to you. But get me the shaving gear first. Then bacon and eggs. Plenty of coffee. Hot, black and strong.'

He was still shaving when the train eased into the small depot. A boy appeared on the platform, a bundle of newspapers under his arm. Brand lowered the window and called the boy over. He tossed him a coin and took the paper. It was a local edition. Thin and flimsy. Brand flung it on the bunk and carried on shaving.

His breakfast arrived and the Negro attendant placed the tray on the drop down table. The smell of fried bacon and fresh coffee did wonders for Brand's mood.

'Here you are, sir,' the attendant said, handing Brand a parcel that held a new shirt and string tie. He gave Brand the change.

Brand thrust a couple of bills into the man's hand as he was leaving.

'Thank you, sir.'

'Something else you could do for me.' He described Lucilla St Clair to the man. 'You seen her?'

The Negro shook his head. 'Don't recall, but I'll look out for her. If she's on board I'll let you know.'

Brand put on the clean shirt and tie,

then sat down to eat. The food was better than he'd expected. Even the coffee tasted good. The only things missing were a cigar and Sarah sitting across the table from him.

The train eased out of the depot a few minutes later.

He told himself to snap out of his somber mood. No matter what he felt about Sarah her fate was out of his hands at the moment. He would return to find her as soon as he could, but his priority now was Beauregard St Clair.

As the train moved out of the depot Brand picked up the newspaper. He wasn't sure why he'd bought the damn thing, or what it might tell him. Which would probably be not a thing. He didn't even know the name of the town where the train had stopped until he checked the front page of the paper. He read it through twice without seeing anything that remotely interested him.

What was taking St Clair to Washington?

And when it came, out of the blue,

Brand cursed himself for missing it.

He was pouring himself the last of the coffee when he froze. Something he'd seen in the newspaper had finally registered. Something he had read and dismissed. He banged the pot down hurriedly and snatched up the paper again.

He was a damned blind fool! The answer had been right in front of his eyes all the time and he'd missed it!

Brand spread the newspaper out before him and re-read the short paragraph printed on the front page. Only a few lines of copy. Black words printed on crude paper. This time, though, they leapt out at him. The words screaming the message that meant a whole lot to Jason Brand right there and then.

EDITORIAL

It has been decided by The Town Council to retain our procedure of past years even though there has been talk of change. *So the Town Band will march to the Church where the Reverend Claypool will deliver the April 14th tribute to the late and still lamented Abraham Lincoln, the then President of these United States, who was Foully Murdered on April 14th, 1865. 'The Flesh May Be Dead And Decayed, But The Spirit Still Lives — And Will Continue To Live — His Sacrifice Will Never Be Forgotten, Nor Allowed To Perish.'*

13

To the west of the tracks the jagged Appalachian mountains lay against a greying sky. A storm was brewing. At the depot on the edge of Atlanta a fresh locomotive was coupled to the front of the train and after an hour's delay they moved off again. Before they had travelled a mile it began to rain.

Brand's compartment attendant reported no sighting of Lucilla St Clair. Brand was certain she was on board somewhere. He was sure of that, just as he was certain she would show herself before they reached Washington.

In the event it wasn't Lucilla herself who came. The door to Brand's compartment opened and a man stepped inside. It was a considerable feat, seeing he was well over six feet six in height and almost as wide. He closed the door and leaned against it, a device far superior to any manmade lock.

'You sure you got the right compartment?' Brand asked.

The man nodded. He looked to be all muscle, without an ounce of spare fat on him.

'I'm sure, Mister Brand.' He raised his right hand to reveal a massive revolver that must have been tailor made for his huge paw. The muzzle of the gun made Brand think of a small cannon. The big man smiled a friendly smile. 'Let's do this the easy way. Hand over both your guns and we'll take a walk. There's a lady wants to see you pretty bad.'

Brand handed over his weapons and watched them vanish into a coat pocket large enough to hide a scattergun.

'You're the boss,' Brand said.

'Out the door and take a left.'

They passed along the train, feeling the rocking of the coaches as they were buffeted by the heavy storm. Brand counted his way through four coaches before the muzzle of the hand cannon nudged him to a stop outside a compartment door.

'Inside.'

Brand shoved the door open and stepped into a Pullman compartment that reminded him of the one he'd had his meeting with McCord in. The door thudded shut behind him, a key turning in the lock.

'How nice of you to join me, Jason.'

There was no mistaking the silky tone of the voice. Brand watched as Lucilla St Clair rose from the velvet couch. Her fair hair was down and she wore a sheer gown that revealed every detail of her lush young body.

'Hard to resist your kind of invitation,' Brand observed, glancing at the man-mountain standing to one side and behind him.

Lucilla laughed softly. 'Elmo has such winning ways.' She smiled at the big man, and Brand saw the devotion that shone in his eyes. 'Elmo, bring our guest a drink. What would you like?'

'Whisky.'

'I should be angry with you. Blowing up daddy's guns and all. I tell you, Jason, he's awful mad at you.'

Brand took the drink Elmo brought him and watched the large figure retreat to a corner of the compartment.

'He sleep at the foot of your bed too?'

She laughed again. The tone was light, her mood frivolous, but under it all she was hard as steel. As she moved the thin gown clung to her breasts, showing the rise of her nipples.

'I guess you must be pretty annoyed with those poor bastards you hired back in New Orleans.'

Her mood changed abruptly. 'They should have killed you. I paid them good money.'

'They won't be needing it where they are now.'

Her eyes flashed. 'You killed them? All three?'

The whisky in Brand's glass suddenly turned sour. *God what a bitch she was!*

'I killed that damned brother of yours as well,' he snapped, wanting to hurt her. 'How about that for a laugh?'

'Willard? Don't expect me to lose any sleep over him. You did us all a favour there.'

Brand flung aside the glass. He sensed Elmo starting to get up and waved the man back with his hand.

'All right, Lucilla, let's cut out the games. You only had me brought here because you found out your hired guns didn't earn their pay. Figure to do it yourself? Make sure this time because it's the only way you'll stop me going after that crazy old man of yours. I know what he's up to. But it won't happen. I already sent a telegraph to Washington. By now the President will be under so much protection even his own mother wouldn't recognise him.'

He saw her lovely face harden. Even so he was too slow to avoid her hand as it struck out at him. The slap was hard, stinging his cheek. He responded without thinking, slapping her back and she stumbled away with a little cry. The sound brought Elmo up out of his chair.

'*No, Elmo!* Leave him. I'll tell you when,' Lucilla said, touching her fingers to the red palm print on her cheek.

Brand watched her, not trusting her for a second.

She turned and crossed to a door. It stood part way open and Brand saw it was the sleeping compartment.

'Come here,' Lucilla said. 'You may as well. You don't have any other place to go.'

Brand joined her. He saw Elmo watching him. The big man's face was dark with anger.

'Stay outside,' Lucilla told him. 'When he comes back out you can kill him.' She eased the door shut and locked it.

'What are you going to do?' Brand asked lightly. 'Convert me to the Brotherhood?'

'I took a liking to you the first time I saw you. It's a pity we didn't have the opportunity to get to know each other better.'

'You figure *now* is the right time?'

'Why not? Look on it as me granting you your last request.'

'I might prefer a good cigar.'

Lucilla's eyes glazed with anger. She stiffened as she stared him out, realising he had just as strong a will. Then she relaxed, and without hesitating she loosened the tie of the gown and shrugged it off. Despite his situation Brand was stirred by her beauty. No doubt about it, Lucilla was a flower of the South. He seized the moment to admire her sleek, creamy nakedness. His interest seemed to transmit itself to Lucilla and she shivered softly, the tips of her full breasts rising even as he watched, long thighs moving slightly as she swayed before him.

'Still prefer that cigar?' she asked gently.

Brand smiled, moving towards her. 'Hell no,' he said.

Lucilla leaned in closer, eyes half

closing in anticipation, mouth curving moistly. And that was when Brand hit her. His right fist came up hard and fast, a short, clipping punch that caught her on the curve of her soft jaw. She fell back across the bed without a sound, sprawling in what might have been wanton desire, legs crookedly apart. Brand shook his head at the sight, thinking what might have been in any other situation. He snapped out of his daydream and rolled Lucilla across the bed. Using handy items of her own clothing he bound her hands and feet and gagged her, then draped the sheet over her delightful body.

He quickly searched the compartment, looking for anything that might double as a weapon. What he needed was a damned arsenal. He had to settle for a six-inch, slim letter opener he found in Lucilla's writing case, wondering if it would actually pierce the thick skin of the man waiting outside. He knew there was only one way to find out.

He unlocked the door and eased it

open a fraction. At first he was unable to spot Elmo, then he saw the man perched on a chair to the left of the door. He seemed to be staring off into space, but Brand wasn't fooled. Elmo was going to be one tough *hombre* to handle.

He threw the door open and went through quickly, turning in Elmo's direction. As he closed on the man Brand drove his left foot up, the heel of his boot smashing into Elmo's side with stunning force. He heard ribs crack as Elmo was driven off the chair. A pained roar exploded from Elmo's throat as he hit the floor. Brand didn't waste the opportunity. He threw himself across Elmo's broad back, hooking an arm around the man's thick, muscled neck, pulling Elmo's head to one side. Then he drove the blade of the slim knife into the exposed flesh. Blood spurted and Elmo roared in pain, his huge body thrashing about as he tried to rid himself of the thing on his back. Brand coiled his legs around Elmo's body, repeatedly stabbing the knife into Elmo's corded neck, feeling flesh and sinew part under the blade. More blood, hot and thick, gushed across his hands, spurting onto his shirt. Elmo still struggled. The man's strength was impressive. He rolled suddenly, arching his body, throwing Brand to the floor, his great weight slamming down across Brand. It was like being crushed under a great rock. Brand lost his grip on Elmo's bloody neck and he knew he was in for trouble if the man recovered fully. The pair of them rose to their feet in the same moment, Brand back-pedalling to get himself away from Elmo.

Upright Elmo advanced slowly. Blood was coursing down his neck, soaking his shirt and coat. He held his head to one side, trying to ease the hurt.

Brand let him come. He had no intention of allowing Elmo to chase him back and forth across the compartment. He held the knife in his right hand, slightly away from his body, waiting his chance.

When Elmo did make his move his agility caught Brand off guard. He lunged forward, turning slightly, then looped a massive fist out of nowhere. It caught Brand across the side of the head and knocked him the length of the compartment. He slammed up against the wall with a solid crash, blacking out for a moment, and Elmo was on him in an instant. His hands clamped around Brand's throat, fingers gripping like steel rods. Brand was unable to breathe, he felt himself lifted off the floor. His vision swam. When it cleared he was staring into Elmo's grimacing face. Brand was close enough to see the blood still pulsing out of the jagged wounds in Elmo's neck.

How the hell was the man still able to move?

Brand didn't struggle, attempting to conserve his energy. The air in his lungs was all he had and wasting it by thrashing around wasn't the wisest thing to do.

That was when he remembered he was still holding the knife. Sticky with Elmo's blood it clung to his palm and fingers. Knowing it was going to be his last chance Brand drew back his hand, hoping his aim was correct, then put everything he had in a single, desperate thrust, shoving the slim blade up and forward. He felt it cut through cloth and then flesh. For an instant it stuck, then sank in up to the hilt. A burst of hot blood gushed out from the wound. Brand yanked the knife out and stabbed again, this time ripping the blade upwards as it slid into Elmo's soft flesh.

Elmo screamed. A high, wailing sound. His hands released their grip on Brand's throat, letting him fall to his feet. As Brand sucked air into his burning lungs he saw Elmo backing away, his massive hands clamped over the handle of the knife protruding from his body. Blood was pulsing between his fingers, soaking his shirt and pants.

There was an expression of pure terror on Elmo's face. His fingers fumbled around the knife's bloody handle, but he seemed terrified of trying to remove it. He stumbled suddenly, falling back against a table. Held there for a moment he began to slither along its length and fell to the floor, twisting so that he landed face down. The impact shoved the knife in deeper and Elmo screamed once, loudly, his massive body arching in a spasm. Blood spread out from under his collapsed body as he slumped. There was a moment when Brand thought the man was already dead. Then Elmo moved slowly, pushing up on one arm, the other dragging the bulky shape of his revolver into sight.

Brand saw the muzzle rise and threw himself to one side, hoping to move out of Elmo's field of vision. The massive revolver boomed once, the bullet catching Brand's left side. The impact spun him round, slamming him against the side of the compartment. He fell to his knees, then onto his face. Even lying down he could feel the coach twisting in ever-increasing circles. And then he blacked out.

He wasn't sure how long he'd been unconscious. He felt weak so he lay still, listening to the rattle of the moving train. Rain was drumming against the roof and windows. Brand sat up carefully, aware of the nagging burn of pain in his side. He leaned against the side of the coach, staring around the compartment.

Elmo lay where he had fallen. His eyes were open, glazed over. His slack mouth was bloody. The big revolver was still clutched in his fingers at the end of his extended arm.

Brand climbed to his feet, careful not to re-open the wound in his side where the bullet had torn a ragged gouge. He'd been lucky. Any deeper and it would have shattered his ribs. The congealed blood had staunched the flow and Brand didn't want to start it again.

He crossed to the door of Lucilla's compartment. She was still on the bed, but from the state of the sheet he'd draped across her she had been trying to move. All she had done was to expose herself. Her eyes blazed with hate as she watched him enter the compartment. He leaned over to stroke her silky hair and she jerked her head aside, muffled sound coming from behind the gag he'd placed across her mouth.

'A while ago you couldn't wait for me to sample your southern charms,' Brand said dryly. 'Something make you change your mind?'

He removed the gag, stepping back quickly as Lucilla spat at him.

'One thing you St Clairs have in common. Every one of you is a fighting fool.'

'Go to hell,' Lucilla snapped. 'Where's Elmo?'

'Lying out there making a mess all over the carpet.'

Lucilla stared at him. 'Dead?'

'I'd say so.'

He turned to leave.

'Wait!' Lucilla cried. 'You can't leave me here like this.

Brand's eyes mocked her.

'Don't bet money on it.'

He took the key and locked the compartment door, ignoring Lucilla's alternating rage and pleading. Brand paused beside Elmo's body and took back his guns. Then he left the compartment and returned to his own and rang for the attendant. When the man arrived he took one look at Brand's condition and shook his head sadly.

'I sure don't know what your business is, mister, but it's the roughest I ever saw.'

Brand managed a lopsided grin. He was starting to feel weak. He peeled off his coat.

'Can you get me something to clean this mess up. And some bandages. Could do with a drink as well.'

The Negro turned to go, then paused.

'Maybe you need to talk with the conductor too?'

'Yeah. Ask him to come see me.'

'You be wanting breakfast?'

'Sounds good.'

'You will be around to eat it?'

'Hell I hope so. Business is over for the day, you can go get some sleep after you bring me my stuff.'

The attendant shook his head. '*Sleep?* Mister, I'll never sleep again after this trip.'

He left Brand alone. In the silence thoughts filled his mind. Of St Clair and his plans. Of Sarah and Lucilla. Of the wild violence that had erupted since his arrival at the St Clair estate and the turmoil that might still occur if he didn't put a stop to the evil schemes of the Brotherhood.

14

McCord was waiting for him at the Washington depot with a closed carriage. On the trip back to the ranch headquarters outside Washington Brand gave a verbal report of the St Clair assignment.

'Any sign of St Clair?' Brand asked.

McCord shook his head. He didn't like having to admit failure. 'Not a sign. Or of Royce. The trouble is St Clair will have friends in Washington only too willing to hide him out.'

'The President?'

McCord's laugh was bitter. 'He insists on carrying on as usual. Just what I expected. He refuses to abandon his duties. I've got our people shadowing him, but you know as well as I do the most difficult thing to do is to prevent someone being killed.'

'What's he doing tomorrow?'

'The fourteenth? During the day normal duties. They'll keep him in the office all day. In the evening he's attending a reception given by the British Ambassador at the Embassy.'

'That would be the most likely place,' Brand said. 'St Clair will need a public place. Somewhere his attempt will attract the most attention.'

'It's the way we're looking at it. The problem is there are going to be over two-hundred guests, as well as kitchen staff and caterers.'

'Add a couple more,' Brand suggested. 'St Clair and Parker Royce.'

'We'll worry about that tomorrow. I'd get some rest, Brand. You look like you need it. And have the doctor check that wound.'

'By the way I left Lucilla St Clair trussed up in her sleeping compartment,' Brand said.

McCord scowled at him. 'I hate to ask what mayhem you created in Louisiana.'

Brand didn't tell him. He preferred

McCord find out for himself. That was his job. Smoothing over the rough edges.

When they arrived at the ranch Brand wandered down to the armoury and had a word with Whitfield. He handed over both his weapons.

'Lost my own Colt,' he explained. 'Picked this up on the way. Handles well but I'd like you to check it over.'

'How's the Special?' Whitfield asked, reaching for the adapted Colt.

'Fine. I'll be needing it tomorrow night.'

Whitfield nodded. 'They'll both be ready.'

Brand visited the ranch medical office. The doctor checked him over and taped up the bullet gouge in his side.

On his way to his quarters Brand met Kito, the martial arts instructor.

'You need work out. In morning before breakfast.'

'Go to hell, you Oriental bastard,' Brand grumbled.

Kito grinned. 'If I do you will meet me at the gates.'

Son of a bitch is probably right, Brand thought.

He reached his quarters and decided to have a long soak before turning in. He fell asleep the moment his head touched the pillow. He slept right through the day, waking in early evening. He had a shave, dressed, and had a good meal. Later he took a walk out to one of the corrals where a sleek chestnut wandered over and stood patiently as he rubbed its neck.

'I was sorry to hear about Lady Sarah.'

It was McCord's voice.

Brand didn't turn around.

'Tell me something,' Brand began.

'I'll save you the trouble of asking,' McCord said. 'I did know Lady Sarah was aquainted with the St Clair's. That she'd met them a couple of times.'

This time Brand did turn around. His sunbrowned face had taken on the look of carved mahogany. 'Never miss a

178

trick, do you, McCord.'

'I can't afford to.'

'Even if it means people getting hurt because they shouldn't be there?'

'That's something we're both guilty of. Think about it, Brand,' McCord said as he turned to leave.

Alone again Brand stared up into the night sky, seeing the cold sparkle of stars scattered across it. He felt empty. More alone than he had for a long time. Part of that was because McCord had been right. They both used people one way or another to get what they wanted. A truth he might want to ignore but one that refused to be brushed aside.

He saddled a horse and rode towards Washington. He felt angry. Bitter. His anger tinged with guilt. He needed a way to forget. The only thing that might do that was a full bottle of whisky.

Two hours later, his head aching from too much cheap liquor he found himself in bed with a striking redhead, striving in vain to prove something to her — though he wasn't certain just what. To her credit the redhead was doing her best to help him out.

'Hey, mister,' she said, her voice reaching Brand through a haze of whisky fumes. 'This isn't doing either of us any good.' She rolled him off her, letting her gaze travel down his body. 'I think something just went and died.'

Brand followed her gaze, smiling crookedly. 'I reckon you're right.' He reached for the bottle on the bedside table and took a long swallow. 'Here's to the dear departed.'

'Mister, that ain't going to help. You down any more of that and it won't just be your pecker that won't be able to stand up.'

Brand flopped over on her, his face pressed into the soft cushions of her full breasts. The girl was wearing a soft, delicate scent that reminded him of Sarah. He raised his head and stared at the redhead's face. His eyes wouldn't focus properly. Her face was blurred now.

'*Sarah!*' he mumbled.

The girl sighed. Her name was Myra. But for the money Brand was paying her she didn't care what he called her. She stroked her fingers through his thick dark hair.

'Honey, do you have a problem,' she said softly, and then with the consumate determination of a professional she went to work on him, refusing to give up without a final try. If nothing else Myra liked a challenge.

Bright sunlight was streaming in through the dusty window of the room when Brand opened his eyes. He groaned. He felt terrible. His head was thick and his mouth felt pasty and sour. He gazed around the room, taking in the cheap furnishings. His clothes were scattered across the bare floor. He sat up, running his hands through his tangled hair.

The door opened then and a redheaded girl came in. She wore a wide smile and nothing else, and her young body was lithe and shapely. She

181

was carrying a tray which she placed on the bedside table. Brand watched her pour coffee into a pair of thick china mugs. She passed him one, then perched her rounded behind on the edge of the bed.

'You feeling better this morning?' she asked.

Brand drank some of the hot coffee. 'Should I need to?' he asked.

Myra laughed, stirring her ample breasts. 'Last night you weren't the best company I've ever had.'

'I give you a hard time?'

This time her laughter filled the room. 'That's the last thing you did.'

Brand emptied the mug and held it out for more coffee. He studied the girl. She was good looking. No more than twenty, with a firm, taut body. If he had been unable to perform to order last night he must have been in a bad way.

They talked for a while, draining the pot of coffee.

'I'll buy you breakfast, Myra,' he said. 'I owe you that much.'

'You paid for more than that,' she said, her eyes promising the delights he had failed to appreciate the night before.

Brand felt a warm stirring and drew the bed sheet aside. Myra gave a slow smile.

'Now that's more like it,' she said as Brand drew her to him. 'But I'm still holding out for that breakfast.'

★ ★ ★

Whitfield had both of Brand's weapons ready on his return to the ranch. The armourer watched as Brand checked the two revolvers, loaded them both and fired off a dozen rounds from each. Whitfield's skills had finely tuned the guns. Brand handled them as if they were part of him, squeezing off shot after shot with pinpoint accuracy.

'The Peacemaker is a nice gun,' Whitfield said.

'Better now you've worked on it,' Brand commented. 'Thanks.'

He took an unopened box of .45 calibre ammunition and returned to his quarters.

McCord appeared a short time later.

'Where the hell did you vanish to last night?' he asked sharply.

Brand laid his weapons out on the clothes chest and opened the ammunition box.

'I needed a break.'

McCord's expression was smug. 'Kito is waiting for you. And that's an order. And don't expect that graze in your side to get you out of it.'

The little Japanese laid into Brand as if he was a mortal enemy. He must have sensed the anger inside Brand and he played on it. He was testing his pupil, and though the instructor made no outward indication he was pleased with the way Brand held his anger in check, channelling his rage into the resistance he offered to Kito's attacks. The session lasted for a full half hour and by the end Brand was bruised and stiff, the bandage on his side stained with blood.

He returned Kito's ceremonial bow and stumbled off the mat.

'Must practice more,' Kito said. He was barely sweating, still smiling, hardly out of breath. 'Improvement is slow. But you are learning.' He gestured to a side door. 'I give massage. Take away stiffness. Make you feel better. Last night too much drink and play with lady. Not good for long life.'

Brand regarded the wiry Japanese instructor.

The hell it isn't, he thought. *It hasn't done me too bad this far and I'm damned if I'm going to change now!*

15

Brand regretted not having Sarah at his side.

The official reception at the British Embassy was made for her. He could imagine her at ease amongst the elegantly dressed and bejewelled women. The men in their finery.

But it was not to be, so he pushed the images to the back of his mind and concentrated on why he *was* here.

He stood at the edge of the crowded ballroom, a slender glass of white wine in his big hand. He wore a new dark suit and boiled white shirt. His tie was neatly arranged, his boots polished to a high gleam, and he felt distinctly uncomfortable.

His eyes were constantly on the move, scanning the mass of people. He was surrounded by movement and noise. At the far end of the ballroom, on a raised dais, sat a British military band, specially brought down from Canada for the evening. Resplendent in scarlet and blue, they played tune after tune with the inborn precision of the British military discipline that was recognised the world over.

The longer he maintained his watch the more Brand realised how difficult his task was. It was hard just keeping track of the President himself, let alone watch out for any sign of impending trouble. McCord still believed in miracles and expected his operatives to bring them off.

The Embassy presented a thousand problems. There were just far too many places for a man to hide. Passages and stairways. Alcoves and quiet corners that simply begged someone to conceal himself. Beauregard St Clair and Parker Royce could be in the building now. Just waiting for the right moment. The precise time to step out start shooting. And McCord would expect, no demand, that Brand prevent it.

He drained his glass furiously.

Damn the man!

What did McCord think he was? Some kind of superhuman? Brand was nothing more than mortal. Able to use a gun maybe better than most, but that didn't give him some higher advantage. Just the ability to kill people.

He spotted a liveried waiter passing with a silver tray holding more glasses of the white wine. He stopped the man and helped himself to a fresh glass.

Back in his position by the wall, watching the President's movements, Brand flexed his shoulders under the restricting jacket of his suit. The Colt Special sat snug against his left armpit. He pondered on whether he would need to use the weapon before the night ended. He was pretty sure the answer would be yes. It seemed to be his destiny to go round shooting people. Brand lifted his wine glass in self mockery. *Here's to the next hundred dead men!*

He watched President Cleveland go

by, waltzing with the beaming wife of some minor Embassy official.

At least the President was enjoying himself.

Putting aside his wine Brand took a slow stroll around the perimeter of the ballroom, checking out the area. Was St Clair watching too? Hidden away in some quiet place. Maybe even now training a rifle on the President? It was impossible to know for certain. Brand raised his gaze to the galleries and niches that ran around the high walls of the ballroom. Too many places for a man to hide. He decided it was time to make another circuit. The President was as safe as he would ever be. Brand wasn't the only one of McCord's operatives watching over the President. McCord had a number of his people spread around the room. Brand knew none of them, nor they him. For all Brand knew McCord's group might include women.

He made his way from the ballroom, almost colliding with a beautiful redhaired woman wearing a green dress. She gave him a fleeting smile as they passed, and he found himself remembering the girl named Myra.

He took the side passage that would bring him to the stairs leading to the gallery that ran around the ballroom. The music faded to soft background noise. Brand slowed his pace as he reached the stairs. He loosened his jacket and eased the Colt in the shoulder holster, climbing the stairs steadily. At the top he paused, checking the shadowed passage that would lead to the gallery, then walked through it.

The gallery was edged by a waist-high balustrade. The crowded ballroom lay some thirty feet below. The music and conversation swelled in volume as Brand leaned against the balustrade, staying in the shadow of a marble pillar. It took him no more than a few seconds to pick out the President. He realised how easy it would be to target the man from here.

Why hadn't McCord sealed off the

entire upper floor?

Brand knew that this was technically British territory, and McCord was unable to use his customary clout. That would not have gone down well with the man. So they had to work within the confines of the concessions the British had granted them.

He decided to make a circuit of the gallery. He slipped the Colt Special into his hand. If trouble did show he wanted to be ready.

Before he'd taken a step he felt fingers pluck at his sleeve, pulling him round. A hard fist sledged into his face, driving him back against the wall and a cold gun muzzle was jammed against his throat.

'Move and I'll blow your head off right here!'

Brand recognised the voice straight off. It was Parker Royce.

'It isn't going to work, Royce,' Brand said.

'But it is working,' Royce said. He moved into view. He was smiling.

Brand checked out the gallery and spotted a shadowy figure at the far end. Leaning forward slightly to reveal the outline of a raised rifle.

It was St Clair, preparing for his moment of glory. His one chance to strike at the President. It would be no more than a one-shot opportunity, because the second he fired the President would be swamped by body-guards, covered and hustled away under a protective umbrella. St Clair would have to make his lone shot count. He would probably be dead himself very quickly after. His grandstand play for the Brotherhood had to be executed without any mistakes.

Which was why Royce was around. His job would be to allow St Clair his moment. Royce had to stop anyone reaching St Clair.

The flaw in the plan was that Royce needed to do it quietly.

He couldn't afford to make any noise that might draw attention to the gallery.

And that meant Brand still had a chance.

'Put the gun away, Royce. You know you can't fire it until that crazy son of a bitch makes his shot.'

The frustration mirrored in Parker Royce's eyes would have been amusing in other circumstances. Brand had been right. His gamble paid off and Royce found himself caught between a rock and a hard place.

Brand moved then, quickly, because Royce would use some alternative means of silencing him if he thought fast enough. It was up to Brand to prevent him reaching that course of action.

He twisted suddenly, reaching up to grab Royce's gunhand, jerking the man's wrist against the natural movement of the bone. Royce gasped as his fingers jerked open and the revolver flew free. Before it hit the floor Brand kneed Royce hard in the groin. The man's breath escaped in a burst. Brand swept up his right hand, the stubby barrel of the Colt Special crunching against Royce's jaw. He stumbled back across the gallery, crashing against the wall, blood gleaming in a dark smear on his jaw. Royce slithered along the wall, attempting to regain his balance. Brand closed in, wanting to end the confrontation quickly. He walked right into Royce's wild kick. The heel of the man's boot slammed into Brand's knee, throwing him sideways. Royce followed him, slamming against Brand and sent him against the balustrade. For a moment Brand was falling into space, his body reacting to the shock. He threw out his free arm and wrapped it around a marble pillar, hauling himself back on his feet. As he faced about he caught a smashing blow from Royce's fist that opened a bloody gash over one eye. The pain galvanised Brand into a powerful response. He flung both arms around the pillar and kicked out with his feet. He connected with Royce's chest as the man rushed at him. The force of Brand's kick pushed Royce across the gallery where he slammed the back of his skull against the wall. Royce grunted briefly as he crashed to the floor and lay still.

Brand moved round the gallery, ignoring the blood that was coursing down his face and soaking the white shirt. He was searching for St Clair, who seemed to have moved from his original position. The man had to be close by. Maybe even now taking aim again.

'Stay away, Brand!'

St Clair appeared at the point where the gallery curved around towards the longer side of the ballroom. He was carrying a long barrelled hunting rifle, fitted with a telescopic sight. The weapon was high-powered. Crafted to be deadly accurate and with the power to drop a deer in full flight.

'It's over, Colonel,' Brand said, knowing his words were falling on deaf ears. St Clair was totally committed. There would be no turning back now.

'Not yet, Brand,' St Clair said. 'This

is a beginning. After tonight the Brotherhood will be triumphant!'

'You crazy son of a bitch, can't you see it's over before it starts. There isn't going to be any damned rising. No Southern victory. Do you think I'm the only one who knows your plans? We have a file on every member of the Brotherhood. The US Secret Service has been on to you for months. My job was to flush you out and by God I did just that!'

St Clair stepped into full view, his rifle fixed on Brand's chest.

'You are lying, Brand, I can see that. Do you think I'm foolish enough to fall for your scare tactics? It won't work. I've been through too much to be frightened off by Yankee trash.' St Clair chuckled dryly. 'First a bullet for that bastard down there. Then one for you!'

St Clair swung the rifle over the balustrade, snapping it to his shoulder. He was sharp, and Brand knew he would have to be fast himself to counter the man's move. St Clair had spent his life with guns. Knew them better than most. But this time he was matched against Jason Brand. No slouch himself where guns were concerned.

Brand snapped up the Colt Special, still hanging at his side, thumbing back the hammer even as the weapon came on line.

St Clair must have seen the move out of the corner of his eye. The rifle changed direction, the muzzle coming round to line up on Brand.

The two shots merged as one.

St Clair's rifle lashed out a crack of sound and Brand felt the clean slice of the bullet cleave his left thigh. He fell back against the balustrade, still keeping St Clair in his line of sight.

He saw the Southerner falter. A spreading splash of blood showed on St Clair's chest.

'*God damn you!*' St Clair whispered through gritted teeth.

He started to lift the sagging rifle again.

'Damn you!' St Clair spat again,

blood trickling from his mouth.

Brand saw the rifle settle on him. He hauled up the Colt, using both hands to steady it and began to fire, emptying the weapon into St Clair's body. Blood erupted from the ragged wounds in St Clair's chest and throat as the heavy bullets punched him back across the gallery. He fell hard, the rifle bouncing from his limp fingers.

The empty Colt dropped from Brand's hand. He heard it clatter to the floor. Then he was down himself. Looking down he saw there was a spreading patch of blood on the floor beneath his leg. More was pulsing out of the wound in his thigh. Now he could hear voices as people crowded up the stairs.

For Christ sake hurry! There's a man bleeding to death up here!

Above the noise, the shouting and the confusion, Brand heard the band start to play again. Restoring order. Placating the disturbed guests. The music drifted up to the gallery and Brand tried to place the tune. He couldn't. He wondered if the President was still dancing, then realised he really didn't give a damn. His own day had been ruined, so why should anyone else have a good time.

McCord was the first to reach him. He clamped a hand over the wound to try and stem the flow of blood. His face was grim.

'What a goddam mess,' he grumbled.

'A simple thanks would have been fine,' Brand whispered, and just before he passed out he was sure he saw McCord smile.

Epilogue

Brand was glad to be away from Washington.

The bullet in his leg had kept him in bed for almost a week. After that he'd said to hell with everything and sneaked away. He'd picked up his old clothes, saddled a horse and had ridden out one evening. He told no one he was leaving, especially McCord. He wanted nothing to do with all the fuss that was still going on in the wake of the fracas at the British Embassy.

It felt good to be back in the saddle, despite the ache in his leg as it healed. The weather was fine, the air fresh, and once clear of Washington he began to feel human again.

McCord could sort out the mess. Him and the politicians. The buck would be passed back and forth until it all got sorted. They didn't need him for that.

Somewhere during all the confusion in the Embassy Parker Royce had slipped away. Free and clear. And so had Lucilla St Clair. She had been under guard in an expensive hotel until someone could decide whether she could be charged with anything. While they debated Lucilla had managed to trick her guard and lock *him* in the room before calmly walking away.

Brand didn't give the matter much thought. He just wanted to reach a town called Blanchville and find a young woman called Sarah.

He took his time, stopping when he felt inclined and moved on when the mood passed. His leg stopped aching and he felt the strength returning to his body as his other, minor wounds healed. He felt his mood lighten as Washington fell behind. Too much had happened during the St Clair assignment. Death and violence seemed to have dominated the case. But McCord had got what he wanted. The Brotherhood was finished and there would be a lot of red faces around the capitol. Brand imagined there would be a number of rapid departures from Washington too.

That lay behind him. The days drifted and the miles passed. And now he was in Louisiana, with a warm sun filtering through the trees edging the narrow road. The scent of bougainvillaea filled the air. Blanchville was no more than a couple of miles ahead. And that meant Sarah. He dug his heels in and felt the horse respond.

The town was small, with white houses and neat fences. Quiet and tidy. A nice place to live.

Brand found the surgery midway along the main street. The shingle hanging over the door read: *William J. Tealer, M.D.* Brand reined in and climbed from the saddle. He tied the horse to the iron ring set in the single hitch post. Stepping up on the board-walk he went inside the surgery. A bell tinkled above the door.

'Be right with you.' The voice was deep and accented.

Tealer was a broad-shouldered man in his forties. Handsome, with dark hair and a strong face.

'Can I help you, sir?' he asked.

'You had a patient brought in a few weeks back. Young woman with a bullet wound. Negro called Frederick, from the St Clair estate brought her.'

Tealer nodded. 'I recall her.' He seemed puzzled by Brand's inquiry. 'What can I tell you?'

'How is she? And where is she?' Brand asked. *Didn't the man understand his request?*

'Are you a relative?'

Brand's impatience swept aside his manners. 'Damnit, man, I've ridden all the way from Washington to find this town. If you need questions answered I'll oblige — but only after I've seen Sarah.'

'Then you haven't heard? God, man, I'm sorry. I didn't realise . . . '

A coldness struck at Brand's stomach. *Heard? Heard what?*

'I did all I could for her. The bullet had done too much damage. Miss Debenham died four days after she was brought here.' Tealer paused, lost for words. 'She did ask for someone named Brand. Jason Brand. Is that you?'

In the long pause that followed Brand heard a voice ask: 'Where is she?'

'The cemetery next to the church,' Tealer said. 'I'll show you.'

Brand was already opening the door.

'I'll find it,' he said over his shoulder. 'Be in to see you before I leave.'

He saw the tall steeple of the church above the trees at the far end of town and began to walk in that direction.

His mind was in turmoil, his body growing numb. He walked along the street, unaware of the curious glances that followed him. His style of clothing and the heavy gun strapped to his waist was out of place in this genteel town. At any other time he might have reacted. Now he was totally unaware. The only thing he saw was the church steeple, framed against the blue sky.

He imagined there would be a green place. Quiet. Dotted with neat mounds, each with its own stone marker.

And there would be one with a name he knew.

Sarah Debenham.

The doctor had said she had asked for him. But he hadn't been there. Not when she really needed him. So she had died alone in a strange town.

Sarah, I'm sorry.

Too little. Too late. It wouldn't matter how many times he said it. She was dead and buried. Nothing would bring her back.

He walked up the long slope that would take him to the cemetery. The white church towered above him.

Brand felt a sting of tears in his eyes. He wiped them away with a brusque gesture. Felt them rise again.

But then it was only the high bright sun flaming into his face as he rounded the side of the church.

That was all.

Wasn't it . . . . . . ?

A TOWN CALLED
TROUBLESOME

John Dyson

Matt Matthews had carved his ranch out of the wild Wyoming frontier. But he had his troubles. The big blow of '86 was catastrophic, with dead beeves littering the plains, and the oncoming winter presaged worse. On top of this, a gang of desperadoes had moved into the Snake River valley, killing, raping and rustling. All Matt can do is to take on the killers single-handed. But will he escape the hail of lead?

RODEO RENEGADE

Ty Kirwan

When English couple Rufus and Nancy Medford inherit a ranch in New Mexico, they find the majority of their neighbours are hostile to strangers. Befriended by only one rancher, and plagued by rustlers, the thought of returning to England is tempting, but needing to prove himself, Rufus is coached as a fighter by a circus sharp shooter, the mysterious Ghost of the Cimarron. But will this be enough to overcome the frightening odds against him?

DEAD IS FOR EVER

Amy Sadler

After rescuing Hope Bennett from the clutches of two trailbums, Sam Carver made a serious mistake. He killed one of the outlaws, and reckoned on collecting the bounty on Lew Daggett. But catching Sam off-guard, Daggett made off with the girl, leaving Sam for dead. However, he was only grazed and once he came to, he set out in search of Hope. When he eventually found her, he was forced into a dramatic showdown with his life on the line.